Brady couldn't help but stare at ne... ..., his heart seemed to kick into overdrive, a fact that caught him completely off guard.

"Calm yourself, man."

He found himself so preoccupied that he almost backed into the mailbox. The tires let out a telltale squeal as he hit the brake. He was thankful he missed the metal box by inches. He didn't, however, miss the attentions of his new neighbor.

The young woman turned and glanced his way with a concerned look on her face. She almost dropped the stack of mail in her hands but managed to hang on to it. Her wrinkled brow relaxed when she realized he was okay, and she flashed a wide smile his way.

Brady remembered seeing that same smile on Abbey's face as she'd talked about her granddaughter earlier today. Now he understood it. This was a girl worth smiling over.

"So you're Bree," he whispered. "You must be something else—to keep such a beautiful expression on your grandmother's face."

JANICE A. THOMPSON is a Christian author from Texas. She has four grown daughters, and the whole family is active in ministry, particularly the arts. Janice is a writer by trade but wears many other hats, as well. She previously taught drama and creative writing at a Christian school of the arts. She also directed a global drama missions team. She currently heads up the elementary department at her church and enjoys public speaking. Janice is passionate about her faith and does all she can to share it with others, which is why she particularly loves writing inspirational novels. Through her stories, she hopes to lead others into a relationship with a loving God.

Books by Janice A. Thompson

HEARTSONG PRESENTS
HP490—A Class of Her Own
HP593—Angel Incognito
HP613—A Chorus of One
HP666—Sweet Charity
HP667—Banking On Love
HP734—Larkspur Dreams – coauthored with Anita Higman
HP754—Red Like Crimson
HP778—The Love Song – coauthored with Anita Higman

White
as Snow

Janice A. Thompson

Heartsong Presents

To Cecilia, the real Gran-Gran
And to my son-in-law Brandon. . .
Who needs football, anyway?

A note from the Author:
I love to hear from my readers! You may correspond with me by writing:

Janice A. Thompson
Author Relations
PO Box 721
Uhrichsville, OH 44683

ISBN 978-1-59789-892-8

WHITE AS SNOW

All scripture quotations, unless otherwise indicated, are taken from the HOLY BIBLE, NEW INTERNATIONAL VERSION®. NIV®. Copyright © 1973, 1978, 1984 by International Bible Society. Used by permission of Zondervan. All rights reserved.

All of the characters and events in this book are fictitious. Any resemblance to actual persons, living or dead, or to actual events is purely coincidental.

Our mission is to publish and distribute inspirational products offering exceptional value and biblical encouragement to the masses.

PRINTED IN THE U.S.A.

prologue

Los Angeles, California

Brianna Nichols shoved the earplugs from her CD player into her ears and settled back against the airplane seat. She willed herself not to think about the life she was leaving behind. What would be the point anyway?

She opted to squeeze her eyes shut instead of sneaking a peek out of the tiny window. With a resolute heart Brianna focused on the music, turning up the volume to a near-deafening level. "Onward and upward." She whispered the words. At least she thought she'd whispered them. With the music blaring in her ears, she must've spoken a little louder than she thought.

"Excuse me?" The businessman next to her turned to give her a quizzical look.

"Oh, uh, never mind." She fought the temptation to explain. No point in doing so. What would she say? That she'd chosen a college halfway across the country to get away from her father? That he was so busy coaching his latest star players he couldn't even make sure she made it to the airport okay? That a lousy move on his part had caused her to lose the only boy she'd ever loved? That she was now headed to Pittsburgh, where she would be living with a grandmother she hadn't seen since she was fourteen?

No, she would skip the story.

And, if she could, she'd skip the rest of her life, too.

one

Pittsburgh, Pennsylvania
Eight Years Later

Brianna unlocked the front door of the duplex she shared with her grandmother, pushed it open and stepped inside. She wriggled out of her lightweight jacket and hung it on the hall tree, then paused for a minute to brush a loose hair out of her face.

"Gran-Gran, where are you?" she called out. When she didn't get an immediate response, fear kicked in. Her grandmother's age and physical condition were top priority these days. Only one thing brought hope. . .the pervasive scent of hot frying grease. Gran-Gran must be cooking again.

Brianna made her way past the collection of silver spoons hanging on the wall in the front foyer, beyond the AGE IS A STATE OF MIND sampler and into the living room, where the furnishings were covered in doilies. No Gran-Gran. She continued on, past the dozens of knickknacks and into the narrow hallway, where her grandmother had created a shrine of sorts out of family photos.

"Gran?" she tried again.

Just then her grandmother's lyrical voice rang out from the back end of the house. "I'm in the kitchen, Bree, working on a feast fit for a king!"

A familiar scent wafted through the hallway, and Brianna smiled as she recognized it—Gran-Gran's fried bread.

"Mmm. I'm coming!"

She entered the kitchen and caught sight of her beautiful grandmother, hair as white as snow pulled up into a tight bun. Her faded yellow-checked apron, the same one Bree had seen her wear hundreds—if not thousands—of times before, made her look a bit more like Aunty Em and a little less like Martha Stewart, but Brianna wouldn't have it any other way. She loved this image of her grandmother and hoped it would remain forever embedded in her heart. She stopped for a moment and closed her eyes to capture it like a photograph, just in case.

Gran-Gran picked up a mound of fleshy-white bread dough from a greased cookie sheet and placed it in a skillet filled with hot oil. Once settled, it sizzled and popped then started to swell. Within seconds the bottom half turned a lovely golden color. Gran-Gran flipped it over with a pair of tongs and scrutinized it. "Not bad, not bad," she said with a girlish laugh.

"Oh, man!" Brianna noticed the platter filled with already-fried circles of bread and snagged one right away. She shoved as much as she could fit into her mouth and talked around it as she asked, "What's the occasion? What's going on?"

Gran-Gran's eyes lit with pure delight. She lifted the piece of bread, now beautifully browned on both sides, and placed it on the platter. She then raised another ball of dough in the air and waved it triumphantly. "Football! The first game of the season is on tonight!" She set the ball of dough in the hot oil, and it began to sizzle right away.

Brianna groaned. How many times had she told Gran-Gran—and everyone else in the city of Pittsburgh, for that matter—that she'd come to Pennsylvania to get away from the sport? But did they listen? Of course not! These Pittsburgh folks were diehards, and Gran-Gran was the leader of the pack. She'd tried for years to indoctrinate Brianna, but, at least so far, the California native remained undaunted. Football and all the hoopla that went with it were a part of her past, not her future. She'd had her fill back in L.A.

"I've been scheming all day." Gran-Gran walked over to the computer on the small desk in front of the window and typed in the Web address for the Steelers, something she did with remarkable ease, considering her eighty-four years. "It's a good thing I'm computer savvy." An impish giggle escaped before she continued. "Those classes at the senior center have worked wonders! I don't know how I'd keep up with the players otherwise. Seems like every year the lineup shifts around on me, and I can't seem to remember one handsome face from another."

"Gran-Gran!"

"Well, the players jump from team to team. Harper's back, ya know. Thought we lost him because of that blown ACL."

"ACL?"

Gran-Gran nodded but didn't explain. "No one thought he'd be able to play this season, but he's back."

"Oh, yeah. I think I heard something about one of Pitts-burgh's players blowing out the ligament of his knee last spring. Football is a dangerous sport. That's just one more reason I—"

"Harper, Bree," Gran-Gran interrupted. "*Harper.* Our star quarterback, remember?" She went off on a tangent about his excellent plays last season before the accident, but lost Brianna a minute or two into her dissertation.

"I think I remember hearing Harper's name from the guys at work or something," Brianna acknowledged with a shrug. "Not really sure."

"Honestly. You're hopeless." Gran-Gran gave her a how-could-you-be-my-blood-kin look. "But since you're stand-ing there, why don't you go ahead and flip that bread over for me?"

Brianna reached to grab the tongs, then gently eased the ever-growing mound of dough over in the hot oil. Noting her grandmother had become engrossed in the computer, she shifted her attentions to the oven, where she discovered something cooking inside. She took advantage of the opportunity to open the oven door.

"Mmm." Gran-Gran's famous meat loaf. After easing the oven door shut, Brianna glanced inside a pot on the stove. Lifting the lid, she discovered homemade mashed potatoes. "Wow. You weren't kidding when you said it was a feast fit for a king, were you?"

"Great football food," her grandmother said with a wink. "Just in case we work up a manly appetite—hollering at the bad plays."

"We?" A gnawing feeling let Brianna know what was coming, even before the words were spoken.

"I've invited a couple of my girlfriends over," Gran-Gran said with a mischievous twinkle in her eye.

Brianna looked up, alarmed. "Who?"

"Rena and Lora. But don't fret now. They've promised to be as good as gold this season." Gran-Gran crossed her heart then kissed the tips of her fingers, as if to offer reassurance. "None of that acting up like last year; they promise."

"Humph." Another piece of bread went into Brianna's mouth, a self-protective measure. If she spoke her mind about Rena and Lora, Gran-Gran might take offense, but the two women—each at least ten years her grandmother's junior—drove Brianna a little crazy with their jerseys, pom-poms, and colorful hand towels. And their play-by-play commentaries didn't help either. She just didn't know how much she could take. Even from up in her bedroom their cheers and jeers proved difficult to ignore.

"Rena's bought a new jersey," Gran-Gran said with a snicker.

"Ordered it from the Internet. She thinks she's one-upped me, but hers isn't signed by Harper."

"Are you serious? A signed jersey costs a fortune. Tell me you didn't. . ."

"I did." Gran-Gran winked. "Bought it from the Internet, but I signed his name myself. Do you think she'll figure it out?" She reached across the desk for the jersey. Across the back, in rather wobbly handwriting, she'd scribbled out *Harper*.

"Oh, no." Brianna slapped herself in the head. "Now you've gone to plotting and scheming. You'll have to do penance for this for sure, Gran-Gran."

"Aw, it's all in fun." Her grandmother turned her sights to her computer again.

Brianna dropped into a chair at the breakfast table and let out a grunt. To her way of thinking, football was a game where a handful of healthy, fit men ran around a field for a couple of hours, watched by millions of folks who could probably use the exercise. A game her father had sacrificed almost everything to—time, family, relationships. The almighty game of football. Yippee.

Wasn't it bad enough she'd had to grow up on the sidelines in L.A., her father off coaching this game or that? Why had she chosen Pittsburgh, of all places, to get away from the sport? In this city, football consumed almost everyone.

She sighed as she thought about the guys at work. Seemed as if they had nothing better to do throughout the winter months than place friendly wagers on the games and gossip over the various players—none of whom interested her in the least. She'd never joined in their chatter and never planned to. In fact, she never planned to participate in football in any form or fashion. . .not since. . .

Daniel's accident. Their senior year.

She shuddered as the memories surfaced, but she quickly pushed them away. She wouldn't think about her old boyfriend tonight. And she wouldn't think about her more recent flash-in-the-pan boyfriend, Andy, either. His fanatical football ways had driven her to the edge. She'd finally put him behind her. Just like Nick. And Matt. And every other Pittsburgh guy she'd ever looked at twice. Not a one of them could see beyond the pigskin to notice she was alive. Maybe they were all like her dad.

"Oh, speaking of news. . ." Gran-Gran glanced up from the computer with a big smile on her face. "Your mother called today to say they're coming out for a visit at Christmastime."

"Really? All of them?" Brianna popped another piece of bread in her mouth. The idea of seeing her mom and brother excited her. Oh, how she wished she could get over the twinge that hit every time she thought about spending time with her father.

"Yes. They would've come for Thanksgiving," Gran-Gran continued, "but your mom said. . ." Her voice drifted off, and Brianna filled in the blank.

Dad can't take time away from the team at that time of year. What else is new?

Just as quickly she offered up a prayer, asking God to help her get beyond these feelings. Maybe her father hadn't changed much since she'd been away, but she had, right? Brianna paused to reflect on the changes in her life since arriving in Pennsylvania. Her commitment to Christ and the teaching she had received from Gran-Gran, Pastor Meyers, and the youth leaders at church afterward did a thorough job of convincing her the past was in the past. . .where it belonged. She'd worked for years to get over the pain of Daniel's rejection after his accident. And she'd worked even harder at forgiving her father for putting Daniel at risk in the first place. Weren't coaches supposed to look out for the best interest of their players?

"Don't look back, Bree," her grandmother always said. "Press on toward the goal."

Yes, she thanked the Lord she had chosen Pittsburgh. She would never have made it this far without Gran-Gran.

Brianna snapped out of her ponderings as her grandmother added, "Your mom said to tell you she's looking forward to meeting your boyfriend."

"Gran-Gran, you know I'm not dating Andy anymore. He never had time for me. That guy is just like every other man I've met since I moved to Pittsburgh. He eats, sleeps, and breathes. . . ."

Brianna didn't say the word.

She didn't dare.

❧

The lights above the field cast a Hollywood-like haze over the players' heads. Watching from the glow of the plasma TV he could no longer afford, Brady Campbell sighed. If only he hadn't told his agent to play hardball with Tampa, maybe he could've settled for a little less pay and no respect. At least then he'd be on the field and not on the sofa. But Tampa had slipped through his fingers this season, and he found himself in the one position any second-string quarterback would hate. Out of the game.

So here he sat, nibbling stale chips, his feet kicked up on the coffee table, watching his former team members on television on a lonely Sunday afternoon. He could only stand a few minutes of outside observation before he had to change the channel. Anything would be better than this.

Ah. The Steelers, playing their first official game of the season. Now *this* would be pure joy. All his life he'd dreamed of playing for Pittsburgh. Maybe someday. . .

Brady kept a watchful eye on Harper, Pittsburgh's star quarterback. The guy had a bad knee, a blown ACL. Despite predictions he'd miss the start of the season, Harper had managed to rehab it and return to the game. Who would've guessed he'd be back this quick? But look at him now, sprinting across the field.

The television camera focused on the scoreboard, and Brady groaned as he reflected on the score: 0-3. "Man." Just two minutes left in the first quarter. Would they rise to the challenge?

Less than sixty seconds later, a yelp rose from the back of his throat as he got his answer. A roar went up from the crowd as Jimmy Harper threw the ball for a touchdown. Tight end Jared Cunningham leaped into the air, catching it in the end zone. For a second it looked as if he might let it slip through his fingers, but tenacity won out, and the scoreboard reflected the shift in power: 6-3. One swift kick later and the electric lights boasted a cheerful 7-3. Not bad for a last-minute attempt. Brady turned up the television to hear the roar of thousands of boisterous fans. How he loved that sound!

A commercial cut into the action, distracting him. Instead of switching back to the Tampa game, Brady swallowed down a mouthful of soda and leaned back against the sofa, contemplating his situation. *Lord, I don't get it. I gave You my life, and I trust You, but it seems like everything is falling apart. How am I going to do all those things You've called me to do if I'm not even in the game?*

He pondered his recent decision to trust Christ as his Savior. That one move had changed everything. And yet nothing seemed to be working out the way he'd hoped.

The commercial ended, and Brady kept a watchful eye on the screen as his old college coach, Ed Carter, cheered on the Steelers from the sidelines. After a few seconds of ego-pumping and strategy planning, the players prepared for the next quarter.

Several minutes in, with the Steelers in possession once again, Harper ran toward the goal, ball in hand. Brady rose to his feet, ready to shout. Just seconds short of reaching the line, however, Harper took a hit, shot backward through the air, and landed on his back. He rolled over to his side, curled up in the fetal position, a look of agony on his face. The referee's whistle blew, and the crowd grew silent.

Brady sat back down, his heart shifting to his toes.

From the way Harper grabbed his knee, Brady knew he was done for.

two

Brianna leaned back against the driver's seat and focused on the road leading out of the North Hills section of Pittsburgh toward the hustle and bustle of the city a few miles south. She turned the nose of her silver SUV onto Interstate 79 and settled in for the trip.

The strains of a familiar worship song filled the air, and she immediately reached to turn up the volume on the radio. As the words took root in her spirit, she joined in, singing at the top of her lungs. In fact, she got so caught up in the lyrics and the beautiful melody that she almost missed the turnoff for 279 South. She managed to catch it just in time.

Worshipping with abandon on the road was not an unfamiliar routine on the drive to Allegheny Building and Design near downtown each morning. Brianna enjoyed this part of her day nearly as much as her time with Gran-Gran in the evenings. And last night's football saga had certainly proven to be entertaining, if nothing else. She was thankful her grandmother's team had won in the end. Seemed like the ladies had a good time, dressed in their jerseys and waving their pennants like high school cheerleaders gone awry.

The song came to an end, and Brianna shifted her thoughts to the day ahead. She sighed as she reflected on the guys in the office. Nearly every one happened to be enamored with the one sport she was trying to avoid. And now that the season had begun, she was sure to hear of little else. Office pools were all the rage, as were arguments over plays and coaching decisions, not to mention the bantering back and forth about incoming and outgoing players.

Brianna interrupted her morning reverie to glance up at the gray skies over the Allegheny River as she crossed one of Pittsburgh's forty bridges into the area known as the Golden Triangle. "Pittsburgh has more bridges than Venice, Italy." She recited the words she'd recently heard a newscaster speak. Still, no amount of bridges could take the place of the breathtaking Pacific Ocean or the beautiful hills of Los Angeles. She still yearned for them in her heart, even though years had passed, and she'd long since reconciled herself to living in Pennsylvania.

"It ain't exactly L.A.," she muttered, as she did almost every morning. "But it's home."

No, Pittsburgh certainly didn't have that Southern California feel. A long way from it, in fact. No movie sets. No glitz and glam. No red carpets. No starlets sipping cappuccinos at local coffee shops. No paparazzi perched for the latest shot.

Nope. Pittsburgh was just. . .Pittsburgh. A little on the gray side at times, but awfully pretty when the winter snows turned everything to a glistening white. During that magical season, the trees hung heavy with blankets of snow, their branches dipping lower, lower, as if they might one day touch the ground.

Of course, those same snows often resulted in treacherous driving, but she'd even grown accustomed to that. Almost, anyway.

The people of Pittsburgh were amazing—that she had learned very quickly. Brianna had fallen in love with their tenacity, their spirit. And she had certainly never met more dedicated business owners than John and Roger Stevenson, her bosses at AB&D.

She smiled, even now, as she thought about them. The brothers, both in their sixties, did a fine job of managing the company and had built it into Pittsburgh's leading high-end home remodeling company. How she enjoyed working alongside them.

Brianna's heart swelled as she thought about that. Her business degree, coupled with her love of people, had served the company well. Seemed like no matter where she went—the grocery store, the auto repair shop, the mall—it didn't matter. She always managed to run into potential customers—folks looking for a reputable home remodeling company. She carried business cards with her at all times, just in case. And her in-office skills had proven to benefit the company as well. It hadn't taken long for John and Roger to promote her to a nicer office space in the building.

She inched her way along in traffic. Off in the distance she caught a glimpse of the area where Three Rivers Stadium used to stand. As much as she avoided all things related to football, it was a bit sad to know that the once-architectural wonder had lived out its glory years only to be imploded when the need for a new stadium had arisen. For a moment she allowed herself to think about Daniel and all he had lost in one night so many years ago. A little shiver ran down her spine as she contemplated how truly temporary the things of this world could be.

She shook off the memory and focused on more positive things. With a determined spirit, Brianna turned up the radio and sang at the top of her lungs.

❧

Brady received the call from his agent, Sal Galloway, a little before ten in the morning.

"Bad news for Harper means good news for you," Sal said. "Pack a bag. You've got to be in Pittsburgh tomorrow at eleven."

"W—what? I'm playing for Pittsburgh?"

"Well, not officially. But they want to talk to you, so start packing."

Brady's heart went into overdrive. For a moment. As excited as he felt about the upcoming news, he knew it came as a result of an injury to another player.

"I don't understand. . . ," he started. "How? Is Carter behind this?" Surely his old coach hadn't put his neck on the line for a virtual unknown like Brady Campbell.

"Carter got you the interview, but I'm gonna get you the job."

After a few brief instructions Sal hung up. Brady held the phone in his hand, completely stunned. He thought about his bond with Coach Carter back in his college days and marveled at the fact that God appeared to be bringing things full circle. He also laughed as he thought about Sal's words: "*Carter got you the interview, but I'm gonna get you the job.*"

"You're wrong, Sal," Brady said to the empty room. "*You're* not gonna get me this job. *God's* gonna get me this job—if that's His plan."

With joy filling his heart, he started packing his bag. He hoped by tomorrow afternoon he'd be packing far more than that.

three

Brianna arrived home from work on Wednesday afternoon to find Gran-Gran at work, trimming bushes along the front of their duplex.

"Gran-Gran! You don't need to do that. I told you I'd be happy to hire someone to do the yard work."

"Pooh. You know I love to work in the yard. Makes me feel young." Her grandmother turned and gave her a wink. "And keeps me in shape."

"Still. . ."

"I'm trying to get the house ready," Gran-Gran explained. "We're getting a new neighbor."

"We are?" Brianna turned to look at the twin unit. It had been empty for weeks, though a host of Realtors had brought a few people by. "How do you know?"

"The sign is gone," her grandmother said.

Brianna glanced at the spot where the FOR RENT sign used to be. "Ah, you're right."

"And I saw the most handsome man today," Gran-Gran said with a giggle. "I do hope he's the new renter, not a Realtor or something."

Brianna laughed. "Are you looking for Mr. Right, Gran-Gran?"

"Not for me!" Her grandmother giggled. "This one was your age."

"Oh, no, you don't. Not again." Brianna shook her head, trying to push any such ideas out of her grandmother's head.

"But this one's different."

19

"That's what you said about Andy. And Nick. And Matt. Remember?"

"Well, I can't get it right every time, Bree."

"At least I knew those guys," Brianna said. "We don't know a thing about this one. What if he turns out to be the last person on planet Earth God would have in mind for me? Then what? I'm stuck living next door to him for who knows how long."

"Oh, he's only signed a six-month lease," Gran-Gran said. "I asked Mrs. Brandt across the street."

"How did she know?"

"Her daughter works as a receptionist at the Realtor's office."

"Have you stooped to spying?" Brianna asked.

"If it means finding you a husband, maybe!" Gran-Gran went back to trimming bushes, and Brianna chuckled as she turned to give the twin unit a glance.

So they had a new neighbor—a man, at that. Though she hated to admit it, Brianna did feel better knowing someone would be so close by, just in case.

She hoped, whoever he was, he'd have a fondness for white-haired women and homemade bread.

෴

Early Friday morning Brady pointed the movers in the direction of the upstairs bedroom. "Watch your step!" he called out, as the two rotund, whiskery fellows rounded the corner with a chest of drawers in tow. Even with his imagination in play, Brady couldn't picture how both of their bellies could possibly fit into the stairwell with the dresser wedged between them. Surely disaster lay ahead.

"Oh, please be careful," he pleaded. "That's been in the family for—" He never got to say "years." The deafening scrape of wood against Sheetrock made him cringe. He looked up to find a gash in the wall, then turned and closed his eyes.

The older man let an expletive fly, and the younger one lost his grip on the tail end of the dresser, nearly causing the family heirloom to tumble to the floor. Nearly.

Brady drew in three deep breaths and walked in the opposite direction, something his mother had taught him to do as a child. How many deliberate breaths had he taken this morning? Thirty? Sixty?

The doorbell rang, mercifully distracting Brady from the scene of the crime. He chugged across the living room, nearly tripping over the large metal dolly the movers had deposited in the middle of the floor—a potential death trap. He caught his balance and continued on beyond a half dozen boxes, past the stack of wall art to open the front door, ready to argue with the man from the electric company on the opposite side. He was supposed to have been there yesterday.

To his surprise an elderly woman—certainly no more than five feet tall—stood on the other side of the door, her white hair coiled up like a mound of pasta atop her head, her whimsical blue eyes twinkling with mischief.

"Hello, neighbor!" she called out in a singsongy voice. "I'm Abbey Nichols. Live next door. Hope you're hungry."

He was. But he wasn't quite sure what that had to do with anything. Until he noticed the plate in her hand. A familiar, tempting smell wafted up to greet him. As Brady glanced down beyond the clear plastic wrap, he noticed pot roast, potatoes, and carrots. And yeast rolls! Just the sight of them made his mouth water.

"Um, I'm Brady," he stammered. "Brady Campbell."

"The name suits you." The older woman took a step in his direction, and he swung the door wide to allow her to enter. Whether he wanted it or not, company had arrived. "I'll just take this to the kitchen." She took a step in that direction, then very nearly tripped over a box. "Can't see the forest for all the trees in here."

"Sorry." He moved a box of his favorite CDs and DVDs to clear a pathway for her.

Just then Mutt and Jeff plodded down the stairs and headed for the door. They stopped short when they saw the plate in her hand.

"Looks mighty good," the first one said with longing in his eyes.

"A man could work up quite an appetite unloading furniture," the second one added as he rubbed his bristly chin.

"Well, you fellas take a load off!" Abbey's voice dripped like honey. "I've got plenty more where that came from. Just sit right down, and I'll be back in a few minutes with two more plates."

She headed for the door, and Brady groaned. How could he tell her he was paying these guys by the hour without hurting her feelings?

The men tipped their caps in her direction then entered the kitchen and plopped down at the table. Abbey disappeared out the front door, assuring them she would return not just with dinner but dessert as well. "Apple pie!" she sang out.

Brady shook his head and whispered a prayer for patience before joining the movers in the kitchen. *Help me to be nice about this, Lord. I'm not sure I can do it on my own.*

He offered the men—whose names turned out to be Jake and Lenny—cans of soda, which they took willingly. Abbey returned moments later, not even bothering to ring the bell. She pressed her way into the room with a smile that seemed to light up the place like the football field at halftime. After passing out the plates, she insisted they join hands and pray.

"You do the honors, young man," she said with a nod. "It'll do you good to chat with the Almighty."

Brady didn't bother to mention that he'd chatted with Him every day for the past eight months. Didn't figure it was the right time. Instead he bowed his head and offered up a quick prayer.

Then the feast began.

Jake and Lenny dove in, barely pausing between bites to say a thing. That left the floor wide open—for Abbey.

"Tell me about yourself, Brady," she encouraged him.

"What would you like to know?" He broke off a piece of the warm yeast roll and stuck it in his mouth.

"Well, it's obvious you're not from the North—that's sure and certain." Abbey laughed. "Where do you hail from, young man?" She gave him an inquisitive look.

"I'm from Tampa," he managed through the mouthful of bread. He pointed at the plate. "This is good. Makes me miss my mom's cooking."

"I do love to cook," she said with a grin. "I'm especially fond of breads. I doubt Bree and I will ever go hungry."

"Bree?"

"Ah." Abbey's smile seemed to widen, if that were even possible. "My granddaughter. She's lived with me since she was eighteen. She's a transplant, too. From L.A. But she's fallen in love with Pittsburgh." Here her excitement seemed to wane a bit. "Least *most* things about Pittsburgh. But she'll come around on the rest."

Brady was just about to ask for details when Jake and Lenny nodded in the direction of the apple pie. "Do you mind?" Jake asked.

"Be my guest." Abbey pushed the pie in his direction. "I'm planning to bake a chocolate cake for tonight." She nodded in Brady's direction. "These are just leftovers from last night. Would've gone to waste if I hadn't noticed the moving truck out front."

Brady nodded then glanced at his watch. So much for hoping these guys would finish up quickly. Looked as if he'd be writing a heftier check than planned.

As he took another bite of pot roast and leaned back in his chair, contentment washed over him.

Really, what did it matter? Even if he had to pay them for an extra hour, it would be worth it for this meal.

With a smile on his face and genuine peace in his heart, Brady settled in for a long chat with his new neighbor.

four

Later that evening Brady caught a glimpse of Abbey's grand-daughter for the first time. As he pulled his car out of the driveway, he noticed a tall, slender blond making her way toward the front door of the adjoining house. She wore a pair of jeans and a soft blue sweater that accentuated her narrow waist.

She turned to pull keys from her bag, and he managed to get a good look at her face. Large eyes. Tipped-up nose. In many ways she reminded him of Abbey. Except for the height, of course.

What was her name again? Ah, yes. Bree.

He gave her another look. She didn't seem terribly made-up, like so many of the women who hung around the players. No, this one had more of a girl-next-door appearance about her. Ironic. He loved the fact that a few wholesome girls were still out there. In his line of work. . .

No, he wouldn't go there.

The setting sun cast an angelic glow above Bree's head. The beauty tossed her blond hair back as she balanced mail in one hand and used the key to open the front door with the other.

Brady couldn't help but stare at her. In fact, his heart seemed to kick into overdrive, a fact that caught him completely off guard.

"Calm yourself, man."

He found himself so preoccupied that he almost backed into the mailbox. The tires let out a telltale squeal as he hit the brake. Thankfully, he missed the metal box by inches. He didn't, however, miss the attentions of his new neighbor.

The young woman turned and glanced his way with a concerned look on her face. She almost dropped the stack of mail in her hands but managed to hang on to it. Her wrinkled brow relaxed when she realized he was okay, and she flashed a wide smile his way.

Brady remembered seeing that same smile on Abbey's face as she'd talked about her granddaughter earlier today. Now he understood it. This was a girl worth smiling over.

"So you're Bree," he whispered. "You must be something else—to keep such a beautiful expression on your grand-mother's face."

She nodded her head in his direction as if she'd heard every word and wanted to chime in with her agreement.

He offered up a slight wave in response, then tried to remember why he'd climbed into the car in the first place. Ah, yes. The grocery store. He needed to purchase groceries to fill his empty pantry. Funny, right now he didn't feel much like shopping. In fact, if he had his way he'd pull his car back into the driveway and head next door to return Abbey's pie pan. Would that look suspicious?

Maybe.

Then again. . .

Brady was so struck by Bree's wholesome beauty and her inviting smile that he couldn't seem to remember how to get the car into gear. In many ways the beautiful blond reminded him of the girls back home in Florida. She looked. . .casual. Laid back.

Why weren't all women like that? Why were so many of the ones he'd found himself interested in so high strung and difficult to please?

Bree gave him a curious look, and he quickly managed to

shift the car into gear. Best to head on out for the evening, not give the impression of a gawking schoolboy. There would be plenty of time to get to know her later. After the news reporters picked up the story of his arrival.

On the other hand...

He gave her one last look as she slipped inside the twin unit. Why it felt as if a piece of his heart remained behind, he could not be sure.

❧

"Gran-Gran?"

As Brianna entered the house, she turned her attention from the new neighbor, handsome as he was, and focused on her grandmother.

"Well, hello, stranger!" Gran-Gran inched her way down the narrow stairs, clutching the rail. Her tightened brow reflected her efforts.

As always, Brianna's heart lurched as she saw her grandmother struggling to make it to the bottom step. "Do you need help?" she asked, rushing to her side.

With the wave of her hand Gran-Gran gave her answer. "Shoo now. Let me do for myself as long as I can, why don't you?"

Brianna feigned offense but then smiled at her grandmother's tenacity. Not every eighty-four-year-old could manage stairs without assistance. Brianna only hoped to be half as spry when she reached that age.

"Have it your way." She offered up an exaggerated shrug as she headed back down again. "But one of these days I'll be calling on you to help me up and down these stairs, and I hope you'll come rushing to my side."

"Oh, pooh." Gran-Gran stepped gingerly down to the bottom step, then reached over for a warm hug, which Brianna returned with great joy.

She glanced up at the sampler on the wall, the adage of which she had memorized less than a week after arriving as a teen. THE OLDEST TREES OFTEN BEAR THE SWEETEST FRUIT. Hadn't made much sense back then, but she certainly understood it now. Some of the sweetest things she'd ever learned had come from this beautiful grandmother of hers.

"Are you hungry?" A little wink followed Gran-Gran's words, which explained the yummy smell in the house. She'd been cooking. Again.

"Mm-hmm." Brianna nodded. "But you're going to make me fat."

"Please. You could stand to put a little meat on your bones. You're skinny as a rail. Sometimes I think you have a hollow leg."

Brianna chuckled. She loved her grandmother's funny sayings. Still, it was a miracle she'd maintained her college weight, what with the great meals placed before her. Not that she would turn any of them down. To do so would be highly insulting to the one person she loved above all others. And, besides, all of this cooking gave her grandmother something to do. It kept her busy.

"Come on into the kitchen, then." Gran-Gran led the way, and within minutes they sat together at the table, enjoying bowls of hearty vegetable soup, made from the leftovers of last night's pot roast. And the chocolate cake looked divine!

"How was your day?" Brianna asked between mouthfuls.

Gran-Gran's brow wrinkled a bit, and concern filled her eyes. Brianna couldn't help but wonder what had put that look on her grandmother's usually cheery face.

"It's that new fella next door." Gran-Gran sighed, and a sad look registered. "Mr. Campbell."

"What about him?" Immediately Brianna's gotta-take-care-of-Gran-Gran antennae elevated.

"Well. . ." Her grandmother reached for her napkin and

twisted it a couple of times. "He's just such a. . .a nuisance."

"Nuisance? He just moved in this morning."

"Yes, but what a day! I've hardly rested since he arrived. He kept that stereo blasting all day long. Hurt my ears something awful. And that dog of his. . ."

"Oh? He has a dog?"

Gran-Gran nodded. "Must be huge. He barked like a maniac all afternoon."

"That's so strange. I haven't heard him." Brianna took another spoonful of the soup as she thought about it. She would need to do something about this if the situation didn't improve. She hated to intrude on a new neighbor, particularly one as handsome as the fellow she'd caught a glimpse of this evening. But with Gran-Gran rattled, someone needed to get involved. And the sooner the better.

"I've lived in this duplex for thirty years and haven't had a minute's trouble with any of my neighbors," her grandmother noted. "Not once. And you know I'm not one to complain about such things."

"Of course not." In fact, Brianna couldn't remember a time when her grandmother had ever spoken a word against anyone in the neighborhood, so this must be very serious. With Gran-Gran's blood pressure running a little on the high side, it wouldn't take much to send it soaring into the danger zone. This rowdy stranger would have to mind his p's and q's if he wanted to go on living next door under peaceable terms.

The wrinkles in her grandmother's forehead deepened further. "I do hope my heart can take the intrusion, Bree."

It didn't take any more than that to convince Brianna. She would take care of this, even if it meant confronting a handsome stranger. Gran-Gran was worth it.

five

The following morning Brianna marched across the lawn and rapped on the stranger's door. When he didn't answer after a minute or so, she turned to double-check something. Yep. Car in the driveway. Likely he'd seen her coming and decided to hide out inside the house. He must suspect an impending confrontation. Or maybe he was still sleeping. It was Saturday morning, after all.

Well, she wouldn't back down. Not that easily.

Brianna knocked again, a little louder this time. She half-expected to hear his dog barking in response. Instead the door swung open, and she found Mr. Trouble with a capital T himself standing on the other side. Wow. He was a lot taller than she'd guessed—at least six feet four—and wider than she might've imagined, too.

No. *Wider* wasn't the right word. He certainly wasn't chubby. Just. . .solid. Especially around the shoulders and upper arms. Did he lift weights? *Man.* She gave him another quick once-over, trying not to be too obvious. Yep. Solid.

Mr. Campbell's face lit into a smile, and she couldn't help but notice his deep, well-placed dimples. And that dark, wavy hair really suited him, too. She blinked hard and gave him a curt nod as she struggled to stay focused.

His opening line caught her off guard. "You're Bree!"

Okay. So he had what turned out to be the richest velvety voice she'd ever heard; so what? She wouldn't let that distract her. Other charmers had tried to get to her in the past, but she had seen beyond them, hadn't she?

"I'm Brady Campbell. It's great to finally meet you." His

emerald-green eyes seemed to come alive with excitement as he reached for her hand, and as she took it Brianna suddenly couldn't remember why she'd stopped by in the first place.

"Yes, well. . . ," she managed, as she tried to collect her thoughts.

"I feel like I already know you."

"You do?"

"Yes, though I half expected you to be Abbey, bringing me a slice of chocolate cake."

How did he know Gran-Gran had baked a cake?

They stood there for a few seconds, his hand, large and calloused, dwarfing her own. Finally she pulled free from his welcoming gesture and attempted to compose herself.

"I, um, really need to talk with you, Mr. Campbell. It's pretty important."

His expression changed immediately. "Of course. Come on in." He gestured for her to join him inside. Did she dare?

She took a tentative step inside. Though his home was the mirror image of her own, the decor was the polar opposite. No knickknacks or doilies. In fact, there didn't appear to be much of anything on the walls, at least not yet. Just a jumbo-sized television set in the corner and a couple of leather sofas.

So. Mr. Trouble with a capital T is a minimalist. Maybe he just couldn't be bothered with decorating.

Just then Brianna noticed the stereo, situated on the wall joining their two houses. Bingo. She looked around for signs of the dog but couldn't find any. Likely he had crated the beast upstairs. Or. . . ,her mind wandered. Maybe the mongrel had taken to roaming around the tiny fenced backyard, digging holes under the fence and scaring children in nearby houses. Regardless, the offending canine would have to be kept under control if he wanted to live in this neighborhood.

Brianna focused on the matter at hand. "Look, Mr. Campbell—"

"Please. Call me Brady." He gave her an inviting smile. She shifted her gaze to the floor, unsure what to make of him.

"Brady. I know you've only just moved in, but I need to talk with you about my grandmother."

A look of concern registered in his eyes. "She's okay, isn't she?"

"Well, physically, yes."

"That's a relief. You had me scared for a minute." He motioned for her to take a seat on the larger of the two brown sofas, which she did. Then he joined her, gazing intently into her eyes as he spoke. "I just love that grandmother of yours. She's completely amazing. Quite a little spitfire for being eighty-four. And a great cook, too—but then again you probably already knew that."

"Well, yes, but—"

"That pot roast was the best I've had in years. And she bakes a mean apple pie."

"Oh? She brought you pie?"

"Yes. Even gave me the recipe. I didn't have the heart to tell her I can't bake my way out of a paper bag." His boyish laugh reverberated around the room, and Brianna couldn't help but smile. "Still," he continued, "those yeast rolls were my favorite. I've never tasted anything like them. Never."

"Yeast rolls?" Hmm. Why hadn't Gran-Gran mentioned any of this?

"Yeah. They were manna straight from heaven." He shrugged. "But I guess I'm giving you the wrong impression. I don't want you to think the food was what drew me in. Abbey has the best personality in town. It's her strong suit, for sure."

"R–right."

"And her stories." He chuckled. "To be honest, she had me laughing till my sides hurt. I could probably tell you anything you wanted to know about almost everyone in your family, right down to naming names on your family tree."

Okay, this was weird. Gran-Gran had talked about one brief visit with Brady Campbell, nothing more. Maybe she'd been trying to butter him up. Regardless, this fellow, kind or not, needed to know what a nuisance he had become.

"She's really won me over," he continued. "And the best part is, she's agreed to pray for me, and I really need that."

"Yes, well, look—I hate to bring this up," she started. "But my grandmother is—"

"Say no more." He jumped up and sprinted to the kitchen, then returned with a pie plate in his hands. "She's missing this, I know. I promised to bring it back to her last night but forgot."

"No, I didn't come about a plate." Brianna shook her head, growing more confused by the moment. "In fact, I didn't even know you and Gran-Gran were this. . .acquainted. I actually came because she seems to be a bit put off by you right now."

"Put off?" He gave her a confused look.

"Perturbed might be a better word," she explained. "And I don't really blame her."

"You don't?" His eyes reflected genuine concern.

Why do they have to be such a great shade of green? Focus, Brianna—focus.

"I'll get right to the point." She stared him straight in the eye, to make sure he understood the severity of her words. "My grandmother's blood pressure has always been a little high. But yesterday, with that stereo of yours blaring—"

"Stereo?"

"And that dog barking nonstop—"

"Dog?"

"All the noise is wearing her out. She can't take it anymore. And since I'm the one responsible for her care, I need you to understand that whatever concerns her, concerns me. So if she's upset by the noise coming from your place, I'm upset, too."

"Well, that would be understandable if—"

Brianna interrupted him by raising her hand. "Look. I don't want to cause unnecessary trouble. That's the last thing I want or need. Gran-Gran and I are great neighbors. Always have been. Ask anyone on the block."

"Well, I never said—"

"I can't remember a time when I've had a run-in of any sort with anyone in the neighborhood, but my grandmother means everything in the world to me, and I'm going to rush to her defense if she's wounded in any way. If anything were to happen to her. . ." Brianna's eyes filled with tears, and she used the back of her hand to swipe them away. After a deep breath, she finished her sentence. "If anything were to happen to her, I don't know what I'd do."

He gave her a blank stare, and she had to wonder at his coldness. Did he not care that her elderly grandmother had been inconvenienced? Was a frail senior citizen's health of no concern to him whatsoever? How could that be, after all the kind things he had said about her? What sort of man was this, anyway?

"So. . ." She rose to her feet and took a couple of steps toward the door. "I've said what I came to say."

"Well, I can see that, but. . ." His eyes, once bright, had darkened with concern.

"No apologies, then?" She stared him down, hoping he would do the right thing.

"I, uh. . .I'm sorry about this. . .misunderstanding."

Misunderstanding?

He handed her the pie plate and muttered a quiet "Please give my regards to Abbey."

Brianna took it from him and turned to walk out the door. The look of sadness on his face almost caused her to turn back at the last minute.

Almost.

❦

Brady pulled back the blinds and peered out the front window as Brianna shot across his lawn, pie plate in hand. She moved away from his house like a woman possessed.

"What was *that* all about?"

He raked his fingers through his hair with his free hand as he thought back over her accusations. Not one of them had been true, though she clearly believed them to be. The only time he'd turned on his stereo since moving into the duplex was late yesterday afternoon when Abbey stopped by for a second time. She'd insisted he play his Frank Sinatra CD for her. Track 3, if memory served him correctly.

Brady smiled as the memory registered. Abbey had waltzed around his living room like a prom queen—alone at first— and then she'd gestured for him to join her.

Okay, so he'd felt awkward whirling around the room, too. In the beginning. But she'd won his heart and eventually his feet.

So why the accusation? And what was all that about a dog? He hadn't owned a dog since junior high school.

At that moment something occurred to Brady, something that almost made him sick to his stomach.

Was it possible. . .could it be. . .that Abbey suffered from delusional thinking? Dementia? That would certainly shed light on her apparent on-again, off-again behavior. Childish and carefree one moment. Frustrated and accusing the next. And it would more than explain Brianna's possessiveness where her grandmother was concerned.

"No way." He shook his head as he contemplated the idea. It would certainly explain a lot, wouldn't it?

As the potential reality set in, Brady released his grip on the blinds. They fell back into place.

If only he could've said the same thing about his heart.

six

Less than an hour after the visit from his neighbor, Brady received the call he'd been waiting for, with news of the all-important press conference.

"We'll make the announcement this afternoon," Coach Carter said. "So be prepared for a media blitz."

"I've had a couple of calls already," Brady acknowledged. "One from a local paper, and another from a cable sports affiliate."

Carter sighed. "You know how this goes. News always leaks out. What did you tell 'em?"

"Just said 'no comment' and hung up."

"Perfect. Just keep it up till after we make the announcement, okay?"

"Of course, Coach."

"Those reporters will get all their questions answered in a few hours anyway," Carter explained. "I hope you're up to the attention."

"I'll manage. Where should I meet you?"

"At the stadium in the press room." Carter went on to explain that Alex Mandel, the team's owner, would be there, as well as Mack Burroughs, general manager. "Be there by 2:15," Carter instructed. "We'll need time to prep and to get you into your new jersey. How does the number seven sound to you?"

"Perfect."

"Great." Carter switched gears. "Did you get the playbook I sent over?"

"Got it."

"Memorize it. Only two days till your first game."

"Yes, sir."

The coach's voice softened slightly. "And Campbell?"

"Yes, Coach?"

"Welcome to Pittsburgh, son."

Brady noticed the cell phone trembled in his hands as he stammered, "Thanks, Coach," then ended the call.

He plopped down on the sofa and began to pray. Words of thanksgiving escaped his lips. They weren't planned or rehearsed but rather flowed out of a heart filled with gratitude. Opportunities like this didn't come along often; he knew that. He would not take this one for granted. And he would use every chance he had to thank God. . .publicly.

A peal of thunder caught his attention, and Brady rose to look out the window. Great. An incoming storm. Well, no problem. He didn't need to leave for a couple of hours.

Minutes later he sorted through his closet in search of something to wear. As he dressed he tried to imagine how the afternoon would go. He could hear it all now. . .the clicking of the cameras, the stirring of the reporters, as the general manager stood and approached the microphone.

"Ladies and gentlemen, I'd like to present the newest member of our team," Mack Burroughs would say. "Number *seven*, Brady Campbell."

Reporters would interrupt with questions, likely wanting to know details of his trek from Tampa to Pittsburgh. They would criticize some of his past plays. Then the real chaos would begin. Those hoping to elevate their ratings would likely stir up old rumors about his wild past and possibly even start a few new ones.

He shuddered as he thought about it. A heaviness filled his chest as he contemplated the past—the man he used to be, the one reporters had chased from bar to bar in Tampa less than a year ago. Rumors—some true and others not so true—had almost destroyed his career and his personal life.

B.C. Before Christ.

Those same initials once represented *his* name—Brady Campbell—but had quickly been replaced with a name far greater. A wave of relief washed over him as he remembered. . . the past was truly in the past.

He hoped Pittsburgh's reporters would leave it there.

Brady showered quickly then dressed for the press conference, careful to look as presentable as possible. Then he called his mother to tell her about the upcoming meeting.

She answered on the third ring, and he opened with the question that always seemed to stir up trouble. "How would you feel about living in Pittsburgh, Mom?"

"It's cold up there."

"Well, yes, but I hear it's beautiful in the winter. And you'll love the bridges."

"It's cold up there," she repeated.

"Yes, but you'll be plenty warm in that new house I'm going to buy for you," he coaxed.

"I'm perfectly happy in my mobile home," she said with a hint of laughter in her voice. "How many times do I have to tell you that? I'd get lost in a big house. Give me something small and quaint any day."

"Still. . ." He hoped to convince her she could learn to love it in Pennsylvania, in spite of her Tuesday canasta group and her Monday/Wednesday date at the YMCA for water aerobics.

He jumped into an explanation of the press conference he would soon attend, and the pride in her voice let him know she cared deeply about all he was going through. As the conversation drew to a close, she offered to pray for him.

"Of course," he agreed.

Not that he could've stopped her. His mama had been known to stop a crowd in a supermarket for a prayer meeting.

Oh, how he missed his mama.

After she wrapped up the prayer, Brady ended the call with the same words he always did: "Love you, Mom."

"I love you, too, Brady. But remember—"

"I know, I know. . ."

They said the words in unison, as always: "It's cold up there."

He snapped his cell phone shut and smiled. One way or another, he would talk her into it.

At 1:30 Brady could wait no longer. The storm appeared to have passed, though the roads were plenty wet. And even though the roads weren't likely to be crowded on a Saturday, he still wanted to leave early.

He grabbed an umbrella and shot out the front door. As he made his way toward the driveway, something—or rather someone—next door caught his eye.

Abbey.

He nodded and smiled but hoped she wouldn't wave him over for a chat. He didn't want to hurt her feelings, but he had no time to visit today.

Hmm. Not that she seemed to notice or care. No, she seemed intent on reaching her mailbox. . .a woman on a mission. Abbey clutched her umbrella in one hand and waved with the other as she made her way toward the metal box at the end of the drive.

Brady climbed into his car and backed out of the driveway. He'd gone no more than a dozen feet or so when he noticed something. He brought the car to a halt and looked around but saw nothing. Abbey had disappeared from view.

He scrambled out, fearing the worst. Right away, he caught a glimpse of Abbey on the ground, her umbrella bouncing across the lawn as the wind picked it up.

Brady sprinted in her direction, rain pelting down and soaking him to the bone. He knew, even before he drew close, that she was in dire straits. Her gut-wrenching cries broke his heart.

"Abbey. I'm here." He knelt down beside her on the driveway, his slacks now soaked. Her left leg appeared to be twisted beneath her in an awkward position, but he knew better than to move her, at least not yet.

She looked up with pain in her eyes. "Oh, Brady!" she cried out. "Look what I've gone and done. I'm such a clumsy old lady!"

"No, you're not. The driveway is slick. It could have happened to anyone. Where does it hurt?"

"My h–hip." Her hands trembled violently, likely as much from fear as pain. Though, from the looks of things, she was clearly in tremendous pain.

"I'm not going to try to move you just yet," he explained. "But if you can, hold on a minute while I get your umbrella."

After locating it and securing it over her, he flipped open his cell phone and dialed 9-1-1. Within seconds an operator came on. He explained their predicament, and the operator assured him help would arrive shortly. In the meantime, she instructed him to keep the patient calm and still.

Not an easy task in the rain or when the patient was in such pain.

All the while he thought about Coach Carter and about Mr. Burroughs. Should he call to say he would be late? Brady glanced at his watch. One forty-five. Surely he could wait until the paramedics arrived and still make it in plenty of time.

"Bree's at the dry cleaners," Abbey said as they waited on the ambulance. "Let me give you her cell number."

Brady entered the number in his phone, then made the call. He quickly explained the situation, and she began to cry at once. "W–where are they t–taking her?"

"Allegheny General, wherever that is."

"I know where it is," Brianna said. "I'll meet you there." She hung up before he could tell her that he couldn't possibly— under any circumstances—meet her there.

Several minutes later the ambulance arrived. The paramedics lifted Abbey, whose face was white with pain, onto a stretcher then placed her into the back of the ambulance.

"We're headed to Allegheny General!" the older one called out to Brady. "We'll meet you in the ER."

"No, I. . . See. . ." He glanced at Abbey's tear-filled eyes and heard her cries.

He sighed as he looked at his watch. One fifty-five. Maybe if he timed this right, he could swing by the hospital on his way to the team headquarters. It was on the way, after all. He hoped.

He followed the ambulance out onto the highway and trailed it into town. They arrived at the emergency room door at exactly 2:03. He hoped Brianna was already here and would take over. Surely she would understand.

❧

Brianna fought the blinding rain as she made her way toward Allegheny General Hospital. The very thing she feared most had actually happened.

"Gran-Gran." Tears filled her eyes, blurring her vision even more. She whispered a prayer—her fifth or sixth since getting in the car.

Brianna swiped at her eyes, determined to remain focused. Her grandmother needed her. A lump rose in her throat as she contemplated the truth of it. *I'm the only one Gran-Gran has.*

Well, unless you counted Brady Campbell.

Hmm. He *had* been kind enough to call the paramedics, then stay with her all the way to the hospital. Maybe he wasn't the ogre she had made him out to be.

Well, no time to think about that right now. With the hospital fully in view, Brianna had only one thing on her mind—getting to her grandmother—and the sooner the better.

seven

At five minutes after two Brady snapped open his cell phone to make the dreaded call.

"Coach Carter, this is Brady."

"Where are you?" Carter bellowed. "We're expecting the media anytime now. Can't do this without you, son."

Brady did his best to explain, but his words were met with hostility.

"What do you mean, you're going to be late? This is your day, Campbell. *Your* day. If you're not here, there *is* no day."

I'm having a day, all right. "You see, sir—"

The team's general manager must have taken the phone away from Carter. "I've already called your agent, Campbell," Burroughs interrupted in a huff. "So if you're holding out for more money—if this is some kind of ploy—"

Brady let out a groan. "No, sir, that's not it at all. This is a true emergency." He went on to tell the story of what had happened to Abbey, hoping against hope Burroughs would find it in his heart to be compassionate. Surely he had a mother or grandmother out there—somewhere.

"You've only been in town a couple of days, and you want me to believe you've already befriended an old woman?" Burroughs snorted. "Just tell me what's really going on here, Campbell. How much more money are you thinking you can weasel out of us?"

Brady drew in a deep breath before answering. "I'm telling you the truth. I was backing out of the driveway in the rain, with every intention of heading toward the stadium, when I saw her fall. No one else was there, so I had to stop."

"Humph." After a pause Burroughs's tone of voice changed. "So you're saying this is weather-related, then."

"Well, yes, I suppose you could say—"

"Where are you now?"

"The emergency room at Allegheny General Hospital."

"Hmm." Burroughs seemed to soften a bit. "Can't exactly do a press conference there, now, can we?"

"No, sir."

"Okay, then here's what we're going to do. We'll tell the press we've filled the empty spot on the line, and, of course, speculations will begin." Here his voice became very business-like. "We'll delay the announcement—tell them our new player was unavoidably detained because of the weather."

"B–but—"

"No buts. And we'll play up the do-gooder thing later, once the story has broken. In the meantime we'll get rid of the media and reschedule for tomorrow—same time, same place."

"Yes, sir."

"Keep a low profile, son. They're going to be on the lookout for you. Just lay low."

"Of course."

"And don't make me come looking for you," Burroughs groused. "I'm going to have a doozy of a time smoothing this one over, as it is. And Campbell—"

"Sir?"

"I'm sending a car for you—tomorrow at 1:00. You *will* be here, understand?"

"Yes, sir."

Brady clicked off, feeling absolutely sick to his stomach. How could this have happened? And yet. . .he peeked inside Abbey's room, saw the pain in her eyes, and asked himself, *What else could I have done?*

❧

Brianna entered the hospital, breathless and terrified. She approached the nurse at the front desk.

"I'm looking for my grandmother. She was brought in about a half hour ago. Her name is Abbey Nichols."

The woman glanced at the computer screen then looked up. "She's in room 3, just through that door," she said, pointing down the hall.

Brianna raced through the double doors and down the hallway until she found the door with the number 3 outside. It was slightly ajar, and she almost pushed it open. Almost. Instead, she came to a grinding halt as she heard Gran-Gran's voice.

"I have a confession to make, Brady." Her grandmother's words were strained. Brianna leaned in with a huge lump in her throat, terrified but not wanting to interrupt.

"What is it, Abbey?" Brady's tender voice took Brianna by surprise.

"I—I've been playing a little prank on Bree."

What?

Gran-Gran giggled, and Brianna almost bolted through the door. Instead she stood as still as a mouse to hear the confession in question. What was her grandmother up to?

"I've been fibbing," Gran-Gran said with a sigh. "I told Bree some things about you that weren't—weren't true."

Oh, dear.

"I had a feeling," Brady responded. "But why?" Brianna could hear the concern in his voice, and remorse suddenly flooded over her for the things she'd said to him just this morning.

"Well. . ." Another giggle erupted from Gran-Gran. "I was trying to be clever, trying to think of a reason to send her over to your place for a visit. I knew from the moment I met you,

you two were perfect for each other."

No!

"Oh, you did, did you?" Brady laughed.

"I wanted her to get to know you."

Tell me you didn't!

"Aha." Now Brady was the one chuckling. "Well, I have to admit, I'm relieved. After she paid me a visit, I racked my brain trying to figure out why you would've told her those things. She thinks I have a dog!"

I don't believe this.

"Sorry, Charlie!" Gran-Gran's giggles took over from there. "But if it will make you feel better, I'll get you one. I have friends at the ASPCA."

"Um, no, thanks."

Brianna decided to break up the party. She cleared her throat. Loudly. She wanted to make an entrance but certainly didn't want them to know she'd heard a word.

"Anyone here?" she called out.

Suddenly Gran-Gran let out an exaggerated whisper, clearly meant for Brady. "It's Bree!" After another second or two she used a much different voice to call, "I'm here, sweet girl! Come in—come in."

Brianna walked in and found her grandmother in the hospital bed. Brady stood at her side, clasping her hand. Though tempted to give Gran-Gran a piece of her mind, she stopped short when she saw the heart monitor and IV drip. That, along with the look of pain on her grandmother's face, was enough to cause her to drop the speech she'd been formulating. She rushed to the bedside and ran her fingers through Gran-Gran's thin wisps of hair.

"What happened?" she managed over the lump in her throat.

"Don't ask me. I was just headed out to get the mail, like

always, and the next thing you knew I was belly-up on the driveway."

"Oh, no." Brianna reached to take her grandmother's free hand in her own, then looked over at Brady. He wore a look of true concern on his face.

"Thank the Lord for Brady," Gran-Gran said, then rested her head back against the pillow. "If he hadn't been there, if he hadn't seen the whole thing—turns out he's a knight in shining armor."

"Um, not exactly." Brady looked embarrassed.

"An angel, then," Gran-Gran said.

At this Brady let out a laugh. "Don't go polishing my halo just yet."

Brianna looked up at their neighbor with newfound compassion. She had been wrong about him in every respect.

"Thank you," she whispered.

He shrugged then looked back at Abbey. "I'm just glad I happened to be there. God put me in the right place at the right time."

Kindhearted *and* a believer? Was it possible?

"I think I saw stars when I hit the ground," Gran-Gran acknowledged. "Then I looked up, and Brady was standing over me. And then I remember seeing the umbrella bouncing down the driveway. Crazy thing had a mind of its own. I think I said something foolhardy to Brady. Something about being a clumsy old woman."

"You're not clumsy," Brianna and Brady spoke in unison, then looked at each other and laughed.

"You just think you're indestructible," Brianna added. "That's all."

Gran-Gran shrugged but then let out a groan as she tried to shift her position in the bed. "I don't feel so indestructible now. I feel like a broken china doll."

"I'm sorry." Brianna gave her a kiss on the forehead, then looked her in the eye. "What have they done for you?"

Brady quickly explained. "They took her back to radiology for a series of X-rays and then started her on an IV drip—antibiotics, as a preventative, and something for the pain."

That would explain the slurred speech and the impromptu giggles.

"But they've got you on a monitor," Brianna noted. "What's up with that?"

"Oh, something about my blood pressure," Gran-Gran said with the wave of a hand. "I guess they were worried about my heart or something. I told 'em to focus on my hip, not my heart."

"Still. . ." Brianna's eyes filled once more. If this episode brought about too much strain, her grandmother's heart could very well be affected. Oh, thank God Brady had been there to take care of her and to make sure she made it to the hospital safely.

"You're going to do exactly as the doctors say, Gran-Gran," Brianna said sternly.

"What are my other options?" Her grandmother managed a weak smile.

Just then the doctor entered the room and introduced himself as Lloyd Peters, an orthopedist. "It looks like you've got quite a break, Mrs. Nichols." He pulled out the X-rays to show them the proof. "Your hip is broken in two places. We're going to have to pin you back together."

"Pin her together?" Brianna and Brady spoke in unison again.

"It's not as bad as it sounds," Dr. Peters explained. "And I've done this surgery dozens of times before. But I do need to make you aware of the risks before we go to the OR."

Gran-Gran nodded, watching him closely.

"Your bones are more brittle than most, due to the osteoporosis," Dr. Peters explained. "But we'll be able to get you fixed up. I'll start by making a surgical incision; then I'll apply metal screws to hold you together while you heal."

He went on to explain things that could go wrong, but Brianna hardly heard a word. Instead everything kind of faded to gray.

Gran-Gran would require surgery. Then a hospital stay for a couple of weeks. Then she would be transferred to a rehab facility to learn to walk again.

Everything inside Brianna wanted to scream. Instead she kept the most hopeful look on her face she could manage, for her grandmother's sake. She needed to play it cool, needed to act as if all of this would turn out just fine.

But would it?

She tried to swallow the lump in her throat and looked away for a moment. *Oh, God, please take care of her. Don't let anything go wrong in the operating room, please.*

After a thorough explanation from the doctor, she headed out into the hallway to chat with the doctor in private. Once there he explained the risks a little more thoroughly.

"Even with surgery the hip might not heal properly. If the nerves or blood vessels leading to the bone were significantly injured during the break, the bone could die."

"W—what can I do for her?"

"She'll be in the hospital for some time, as I said. She will need that lengthy period of bedrest to help the bone heal."

Brianna swallowed hard and nodded. She would make sure Gran-Gran was taken care of. Somehow.

"After that she will be transferred to rehab. Once she's there you will need to encourage her to get up and around. As I mentioned, rehabilitation will be critical to her recovery, so make sure she cooperates."

The doctor wrapped up his instructions then turned, leaving Brianna in stunned silence.

Grief overtook her, and she leaned against the wall, tears streaming. At that very moment she felt a strong arm reach around her shoulders, drawing her into an awkward embrace. She leaned her face into Brady's chest and wept, silently at first, then with unashamed abandon.

When she calmed down she closed her eyes and shook her head. "What am I going to do?"

"We're going to do exactly what she needs us to do," he explained. "Starting with going back in there to spend a few minutes with her before they prep her for surgery. Then we're going to pray." He looked into her eyes. "You heard what the doctor said, Bree. She's going to be okay."

Brianna nodded but didn't feel the same assurance in her heart. Whenever she thought about losing Gran-Gran, fear gripped her. She didn't know how she would make it if—

"Let's go back in the room." Brady interrupted her thoughts. "She's probably missing us by now."

They entered the room to find Gran-Gran with the remote in hand. Her eyes, once filled with pain, now twinkled with delight. "You're never going to believe this!" she said as she turned to look at Brianna.

"What, Gran-Gran?"

"They've got cable TV! I'm watching the sports channel."

Brianna dropped into a chair. "Of all things."

"And get this," Gran-Gran continued with a frustrated look on her face. "All that stuff about a press conference today at 3:00? Baloney! It's been canceled."

Brianna noticed Brady's gaze shift to the floor.

Her grandmother forged ahead, clearly upset about something having to do with a new player. "The fact that he didn't show up for the press conference just confirms what I've been saying all week. In fact, Rena and I argued about this very thing last night. All of this frenzy is a hoax to give fans false hope. We're not getting a new quarterback. All of this media attention is just to sell tickets."

Brianna turned to look at Brady to see if he could make any sense out of Gran-Gran's words. Maybe he understood a little something about football. Clearly she didn't.

As she opened her mouth to ask for his opinion, she glimpsed his face.

For whatever reason, the man looked like a deer caught in the headlights.

eight

Brady paced the tiny OR waiting room with a cup of coffee in his hand. He passed the desk, which sat empty. Off in the distance a wall-hung television flashed photos of a car accident on one of the local highways. No one in the room seemed to be paying much attention to the news. Most were gathered together in huddles, worried looks on their faces. A few sat slumped over in chairs, dozing.

Brady shuddered as he remembered another time, years ago, when he and his mother had gathered with his older siblings in a similar hospital waiting room in Florida. His father had been whisked away into surgery to repair a clogged artery in his neck. Just a minimal procedure, according to the doctors. No big deal.

How long had they waited in the room together, hunkered down, like so many of these folks—two hours? three?—before the doctors came to give them the grim news. Unexpected and horrifying news.

Massive stroke.

Another shiver ran down Brady's spine as he remembered the series of events that followed.

Coma, little hope.

Days of waiting, praying.

His older brother—distant and removed—acting like nothing was wrong.

An ever-present mob of his mother's church friends.

The morning to end all mornings.

Casseroles.

Everything after that one awful day had involved casseroles and older women with white hair moving back and forth in a steady stream from the house, tending to his mother's every need.

Ironically his father had tended to his mother's every need also, even before passing on. Turned out his organizational skills had worked to everyone's advantage. Brady smiled as he remembered the day his mother had pulled out the paperwork. His father had taken care of every detail in advance, right down to writing his own eulogy and obituary and planning the order of service. He'd left nothing to chance, even naming his favorite hymns and selecting a suit to be buried in.

No, James Campbell had left nothing for his wife to deal with after the fact—nothing other than mourning the only man she'd ever loved.

Brady glanced back up at the television and sighed. He hoped today's surgery would in no way be reminiscent of all that. He shook off the memories and turned toward Brianna. She seemed to be holding up pretty well, all things considered. Her tears still flowed intermittently, but who could blame her? She was her grandmother's caregiver, after all, and her love for Abbey was. . .what was that expression Abbey always used? Ah, yes. Sure and certain. Brianna's love for Abbey was sure and certain.

Brady gave Brianna a closer look. Her beauty had been apparent from the get-go, but seeing her here, in this situation—seeing the compassion in her eyes and the concern etched across her brow—made her all the more appealing. This was a girl you could take home to Mama.

Whoa. Slow down. What are you thinking? You just met her.

"Brady?" Brianna interrupted his thoughts as she stood. "I'm going to the gift shop for a few minutes."

"Can I come with you?"

When she nodded, he followed on her heels down the corridor in search of the gift shop. They wound their way through a maze of hallways, observing the signs, until they arrived at the tiny, crammed shop.

Brianna at once began to search for a gift. Her brow wrinkled in concern after just a couple of minutes. "What should I get for her?"

"What does she like?"

Brianna rolled her eyes. "Trust me—they won't have what she *really* likes in here."

Brady wondered at that but didn't ask. "Maybe flowers?" he tried. When Brianna shrugged, he suggested something else. "Candy?"

"I don't know if the doctor will have her on a special diet or not," Brianna said with a sigh.

"Hmm. I see your point." He looked around the room, and his gaze finally came to rest on a bouquet of Mylar balloons. "Hey, what about those?"

As Brianna looked up, a smile lit her face. "Yeah. That's perfect." She made her way to the counter where she ordered a half dozen Get Well and You Are Loved balloons in a variety of colors and shapes.

As the clerk filled the balloons and then rang up her total, Brady found himself distracted by the greeting cards. One in particular caught his eye. It was funny—witty, really—just like Abbey. It even had a dog on front. He carried it to the cash register and paid for it with a grin. "I think she'll like this."

As they left the shop he handed the card to Brianna. As their hands touched, her cheeks flushed, and he grinned. Something about the touch of her hand, even for a moment, felt good. Felt right.

And completely odd. Nothing like this had ever happened to him before.

Brianna took the card and read it, giving him a funny look as she spied the dog, then laughed aloud. She handed it back to him with an admiring gaze. "You really *do* know her well, don't you?"

He shrugged. "Well, I feel like I do. In so many ways she reminds me of my mother. Older, of course. But my mom's no spring chicken. I'm the youngest of four kids, and my siblings are considerably older than I am. I was born when my mom was forty-two."

"You were a surprise package?"

"What?"

Brianna smiled. "That's what my mom always called my younger brother—her little surprise package. He came along years after I did."

Brady nodded. "I guess that about sums it up." He paused for a moment to gather his thoughts. "My parents were ten— maybe even fifteen—years older than my friends' parents, but they were young-acting." He smiled. "My mom is still young at heart. She has a terrific sense of humor, just like Abbey. Even cooks like her."

"Does she live in Pittsburgh?"

"Nope. But I'm working on that. She lives in Florida, but I'm hoping she'll move here before long. My older siblings aren't great at taking care of her. She really depends on me. It's always been like that."

Brianna flashed him a smile. "Did you say you're from Florida?" When he nodded, she delved into a lengthy explanation of how much she missed the beach. "I'm from L.A.," she added.

"Yes, I know—"

"Abbey told you," she finished for him.

When he nodded, Brianna laughed. "If I didn't know any better, I'd have to say my grandmother has been up to some tricks."

"Oh?" He didn't dare reveal any of the things Abbey had shared with him in the emergency room. Instead he glanced over at Brianna to gauge her expression. As he did he noted a hint of a smile on her face. It warmed his heart.

In fact, everything about this girl warmed his heart.

&

Brianna fought the grogginess that seemed to consume her as the hours ticked by in the waiting room. Many times she glanced over at Brady, wondering how long he planned to stay. He'd come in his own car, after all, and could go whenever he liked.

Still, he seemed satisfied to sit next to her, staring at the muted television and occasionally striking up a conversation.

She peeked at him out of the corner of her eye. Surely Brady Campbell had something better to do on a Saturday night than sit around a dreary hospital, waiting for news about a woman he barely knew. But he looked content. Strange.

Why had she disliked him so much? Ah, yes. Because of Gran-Gran.

She grinned as she replayed the conversation she'd overheard between her grandmother and Brady earlier in the day. Funny, how one little thing could change her mind so completely.

"What are you smiling about?"

"W–what?" Brianna looked up into Brady's laughing green eyes. *Who has eyes that gorgeous?* She was embarrassed at having been caught so deep in her thoughts, particularly when most of those thoughts concerned him. "Oh, I—"

"You're smiling," he said.

"Oh? Well. . .I was. . .thinking of Gran-Gran." It wasn't a

lie. She had been thinking of her, hadn't she? And Brady, too, of course, though she wouldn't mention that part.

"I can see why you're smiling," Brady said with a nod. "I'm glad you're feeling better about her surgery. I'm sure she's going to come through this with flying colors."

Brianna nodded. "I know you're right. She's tough as nails most of the time, so it'll be interesting to see how she fares under stress. I'd imagine she'll be a lot of fun to care for. She should be fine, at least on Monday nights."

"Monday nights?" He gave her a curious look.

"Yes, she's quite a football nut. Turn on the game and she's as happy as a lark."

"Oh, really." His eyes lit up, and for a moment she half expected him to jump into an animated play-by-play of last week's game, like almost every other guy she knew. Instead he offered a weak shrug and turned back to the television.

Maybe there was hope for this guy.

Seconds later Dr. Peters entered the room. He looked exhausted but was smiling. "She came through fine," he said. "She's in the recovery room now. We'll be moving her to a private room when she wakes up."

"She—she's going to be okay?" Brianna asked.

The doctor gave her a confident nod. "I have every reason to think she'll do just fine. She's a feisty one, for sure, but that will work to her advantage. She seems to have an indomitable spirit."

"Yes, she does," Brianna agreed.

After a few words of instruction from the doctor, they were escorted to the recovery room, where they found Abbey waking up. She seemed frightened and disoriented. Brianna did her best to soothe and comfort her grandmother, but it took a good hour before she seemed to come around.

A short time later Brianna and Brady followed along

behind the rolling bed as they made their way into a tiny private room at the east end of the hospital. The nurse came to check Gran-Gran's vital signs, then gave her some medication for pain. Within minutes she dozed off into a fitful sleep. Brianna kissed her on the forehead and settled into a nearby chair.

"Aren't you going home?" Brady whispered.

She looked up, confused. "Home?"

"You're not going to stay here all night, are you?"

"Well, yes. That's my plan anyway."

He shook his head. "You need your rest if you're going to take care of her."

Brianna shrugged. "I'll sleep here in the chair."

"This is just my opinion," Brady pointed out, "but I think you'll do a better job of caring for your grandmother if you've had a good night's sleep."

"He's right, you know," Gran-Gran mumbled in a groggy voice.

Brianna groaned and gave Brady an accusing look. "You're saying I should go home? Leave her here?"

"Nurses are on call around the clock," Brady said. "She'll be well taken care of. But if it will make you feel better, you can talk to the head nurse and ask her to call you if there's a problem."

A yawn escaped Brianna's lips. Maybe he was right. Maybe a good night's sleep was in order. Tomorrow was Sunday. She could come back in the morning and stay all day.

"Go home, Bree," Gran-Gran whispered through her medicated fog. "I need my rest. . .and I won't sleep a wink. . . if I know you're sitting over there worrying."

"Fine." Brianna stood up and reached for her jacket. "I'm going home, then."

"Let me drive you," Brady offered.

"Oh, I have my car."

"Leave it. I'll take you home, then follow you back up here in the morning." Her eyes widened, and he added, "I won't be able to stay long tomorrow, but I want to come for a while before heading off to. . .work."

He works on Sunday? What does he do?

"You're a good boy," Gran-Gran muttered in a slurred voice.

Brianna giggled. "I think she's got something there." She looked at Brady with growing admiration. "And I think I'll take you up on your offer. I'm too tired to drive right now anyway."

"All right then."

He leaned over to brush a soft kiss across Gran-Gran's cheek, and she whispered, "You two go on now. Leave me be," in a hoarse voice.

As they walked through the door, Brianna, with tears in her eyes, looked back at her grandmother. She whispered a silent prayer that Gran-Gran would make it through the night without pain, then she stopped at the nurse's station to leave her phone number.

Then, with exhaustion eking from every pore, she followed Brady toward the parking garage.

nine

The next morning Brady awoke with a smile on his face. Might've had something to do with the fact that he'd dreamed about Brianna. In his dream she'd been sitting on the sidelines at the game while he scored a touchdown. The electric lights celebrated his victory, and the roar from the crowd made him feel welcome. Brianna had rushed to his side at the end of the game, slipping easily into his arms. Her kiss had caused more excitement than the touchdown.

Yep. Definitely a dream. But what a nice one.

Brady lingered in bed for a few minutes, praying. He lifted up his mother's name as always. Next he covered his siblings, though praying for his older brother still proved to be a challenge, all things considered. Afterward he prayed for Abbey—for her healing and for her psychological state.

Finally he turned to Brianna.

Hmm. He tried to stay focused on the prayer time but found himself slightly distracted as he remembered the look of pain in her eyes last night at the hospital. How wonderful it had felt to wrap her in his arms, to offer comfort. Something in him wanted to protect her, to kiss away every tear, to tell her everything would be all right.

Best to get back to praying.

He took a few minutes to pray about today's press conference, adding a special request: "Please let Burroughs forgive me for what happened yesterday." If everyone came into today's events with a good attitude, the media would surely pick up on that. Being the new kid in town, he wanted to put his best foot forward.

A short time later Brady climbed out of bed and padded downstairs to the kitchen, where he switched on the coffee-maker. Wouldn't take long for the pot to fill. In the meantime he needed a shower and a shave. As he did that, he laid out a plan of action for the day. What was it Burroughs had said? Ah, yes. "I'll send a car for you at 1:00."

Brady would be waiting at the house. Of course, that meant his visit with Abbey would have to be brief.

He chuckled, thinking of his elderly neighbor. Even heavily medicated, her matchmaking skills were still intact. "You two go on now." Was that what she had said? Surely she'd meant, "You two spend a little more time together. It'll do my heart good."

Not that he minded. No, he'd be happy to spend as much time as possible with Brianna. She did *his* heart good.

Brady headed off to the kitchen, where he popped a slice of bread into the toaster and poured a cup of coffee. As he settled down at the table, he tried to envision Brianna next door, doing the same. For whatever reason he started to chuckle, thinking about the fact that she'd accused him of having a dog—a noisy one, at that. Maybe he should set the record straight today—tell her the dog was nonexistent and the stereo had only been used at Abbey's insistence.

On the other hand, if he shared that little tidbit, she would know Abbey had made up the stories in the first place. From there she would likely guess her grandmother had ulterior motives. *Nope, I won't tell her today.* He didn't want to create a stir, especially not with Abbey in such a fragile state.

Brady glanced down at his watch and realized he'd daydreamed away nearly twenty minutes. He'd promised to meet Brianna at her place at 9:00. Better get on the ball.

❧

As soon as Brianna heard the knock on the door, her heart leaped into her throat. *Brady.* She glanced in the mirror, checking her makeup one last time. Not too bad. The eye shadow on her left eye was a bit heavier than the right, but who would really notice?

She paused to grab a sweater from the closet, then sprinted down the stairs to the door. She answered in a somewhat breathless state. "Good morning." Brianna ushered him inside. "Are you hungry?"

"Well, I, uh. . ." He gave her a puzzled look. "Do we have time?"

"Gran-Gran spent much of yesterday morning baking, so the kitchen is filled with breakfast goodies needing to be eaten. And, besides, we always do a big breakfast on Sunday mornings. It's tradition. So follow me."

She led him down the hallway, chatting all the way. When she didn't hear a response she turned back, stunned to find him still standing in the living room, gazing at her grandmother's spoon collection. She took a few steps back in his direction. He looked around the room, eyes wide.

"I don't believe it," he said.

"Believe what?"

"Well, for one thing, this spoon collection. My mom has one just like it. And the knickknacks. It's just like—like home."

"Ah. Well, it *is* home." She flashed him a warm smile.

"Yes, but how odd that I'd come all the way from Florida to Pittsburgh only to feel so completely at home again." He shrugged. "You know, I'm convinced my mom and Abbey would be good friends. They'd keep each other busy; that's for sure. My mom takes all sorts of classes to stay active."

"Internet courses?"

"Yes, and others, too. Like water aerobics. Arts and crafts. That kind of thing." He chuckled. "She's a real go-getter. And her taste in decorating is pretty much the same, too." He gestured to the sofa. "Let me guess. Abbey has had that couch since the '80s, right?"

"Seventy-nine, according to Gran-Gran," Brianna said with a nod. "And the recliner has been here longer than that. My grandpa used to sit in it every day after work." She grew silent as she thought about it. How long had it been since she'd mentioned her grandfather? He'd died years before she moved to Pittsburgh, leaving Abbey alone—and Brianna with a host of questions about what he must've been like. She'd barely known him, though her grandmother had tried to tell her a little.

She shook off the memory and invited Brady again to join her in the kitchen. There she served up a steaming mug of coffee with French vanilla creamer and sugar. He eyed the large coffee cake in the center of the dinette table. "You weren't kidding. This looks great."

"You should see the cinnamon rolls." She opened the microwave and pulled out a plate of the warm, gooey rolls, covered in frosting.

"How do you eat like this all the time and stay so—?" He didn't finish his sentence. His cheeks reddened and he muttered, "Sorry."

"No, it's okay." She shrugged. "My job is really active. I'm on my feet much of the time. And I take a lot of walks with my grandmother when the weather cooperates. In other words, I burn off all the calories." She smiled. "I'm always telling Gran-Gran to cut back on the shortening and sugar, but the more I tell her, the more she bakes. It's useless."

"Do you cook?"

Brianna shrugged. "I try, but there's no comparison. Gran-Gran got all of the cooking skills in the family. It's kind of a—a gift."

His eyebrows elevated playfully. "One we *all* get to share."

"Yep." As they settled down at the table to enjoy a quick bite to eat, Brianna looked into his eyes—eyes filled with goodness and compassion. How had she missed that the first time around?

"Tell me about your life in L.A.," he coaxed.

"Ah." She drew in a deep breath, wondering where to begin. "My mom is great. She and I have always been close ever since I was little. And my younger brother is a hoot. I think you'd like him. He's a lot younger than I am, so we didn't have a lot in common."

"What about your dad?"

She was quiet for a moment. "My dad and I haven't always seen eye-to-eye," she finally said. "We had a falling-out of sorts when I was eighteen. He did something. . . ." She didn't finish. No point in weighing the conversation down with that. "Anyway, when the time came to make a decision about college, I needed to get away, to clear my head. I opted to come here to live with my grandmother. It opened a world of possibilities to me, and I've never been sorry."

"How are things with your dad now?" Brady asked.

"Oh. . .I don't know," she said with a sigh. "He's just kind of. . .absent. Always has been. He has his priorities, and family is pretty far down on the list."

"I'm sorry to hear that." His gaze shifted downward. "I lost my dad awhile back. It's been really hard without him. I miss him so much."

Ouch.

She drew in a deep breath. "I'm so sorry, Brady. And I don't mean to give you the wrong impression. I love my dad, and I'm working on the relationship with him. I just keep praying and trying."

"That's all the Lord would ask you to do," he said.

"He's not as bad as I've made him out to be, I guess," she said. "And sometimes it's hard to believe he's Gran-Gran's son. They're so opposite." *Well, except for their love of the game.* "She's as soft as butter and loves me as I've never been loved before."

"That's one way to put it." He grinned, then gave her a reflective look.

"What about you?" she asked. "You're a self-proclaimed mama's boy, right?"

His gaze shifted downward, and she had to wonder what was going through his mind.

Just then her cell phone rang, creating a distraction. She reached to open it, startled to hear Gran-Gran's voice on the other end of the line.

"Bree, can you bring me my bathrobe? And my denture case. I had a doozy of a time finding my teeth this morning."

Brianna chuckled. "Of course. Anything else?"

"Well, they've told me I can eat anything I like," her grandmother said. "And I'm missing my Sunday morning feast, so bring some of those cinnamon rolls. And I want my own coffee. Can you bring me a thermos filled to the top?"

"As long as you're sure the doctor won't mind."

"Oh, don't worry about the doctor. He won't mind, but even if he did, I'd tell you to bring it anyway."

"Yes, but I wouldn't—because I love you and care about your health."

Gran-Gran sighed. "You're a good girl, Bree."

Brianna glanced across the table at Brady, and he warmed her heart with his boyish grin. "Is everything okay?" he asked.

"Yeah. She's found her teeth and wants some cinnamon rolls."

"Um, okay." He laughed. "I guess that makes sense in the grand scheme of things. Is she anxious to see you?"

"More anxious to see *you*, I'd be willing to bet."

His eyes twinkled. "Me?"

"Yeah. She's a sucker for a Steelers' fan."

"Steelers' fan?" He looked down at his T-shirt and realized it bore his new team's logo. "Ah."

"Just wait and see," she said with a wink. "Just wait and see."

ten

Brady looked across the hospital room at Abbey, who lay in the bed with a more-serious-than-usual look on her face.

"Everything okay?"

She glanced his way, her eyes filling with tears. At once he stood and joined her at the bedside. "Should I go and find Brianna?"

"No, I'm glad she's stepped out for a minute. I don't want her to see me like this."

"I understand. Would you feel better if I left you alone for a few minutes?" He glanced down at his watch. Eleven forty five. He'd have to leave soon anyway.

"No, please don't go. Pull your chair a little closer so we can chat."

He did as instructed but was still a little startled when Abbey reached for his hand. He offered it willingly.

"Do you pray, Brady?" she asked.

"I do. I've been praying for you. Just this morning, in fact."

"Humph." She shook her head. "I'm just fine. Might make more sense for you to pray for our political leaders or the situation in the Middle East."

"Well, I do that, too."

"I've walked with God a mighty long time," she said with a sigh. "We're like two old friends—God and me, sitting together on the couch, talking."

"I can see that." He gave her hand a squeeze. "It shows that you spend time with Him."

"I might be spending time with Him face-to-face soon," she said softly.

Her words took him by surprise, but he tried not to over-react. Instead he opted for an easygoing approach. "Are you looking forward to that?"

"I'm looking forward to eternity," she said with a smile. "When the time is right. Getting to see my husband, Norman, again. And Katie."

"Katie?"

"My baby girl." She reached up with her fingertips to brush away a loose tear from her lashes. "She passed away when she was only three. Nearly broke my heart in two."

"Oh, I'm so sorry. I didn't know."

Abbey smiled. "Bree was the spitting image of Katie when she was little. And when I look at Bree. . .well, I kind of imagine that's what Katie might've looked like if she'd lived to her twenties. But that's not how things turned out." Her voice softened. "Sometimes things don't go the way you expect them to."

"Right." He couldn't think of anything else to say. He wanted to tell her about his father, how he'd been snatched away too soon, but didn't want to interrupt. This was her time.

"I have so many regrets." Abbey's eyes filled once again.

Brady spoke with tenderness. "What kind of regrets?"

Her lip quivered, and she didn't answer for a moment.

"My oldest son—Bree's father—we've never been very close. I wish I could change that."

Her revelation seemed to match Brianna's earlier description of her "absent" father.

"Maybe he'll come around," Brady encouraged. "Just keep praying."

"He's so much like his father that it hurts," she said. "My

husband, Norman, was distant, not around much. When he did come home, he seemed set on getting his own way most of the time." She paused and shook her head. "Really *all* of the time. He didn't like to take no for an answer. And when Glen came along I could see they were two peas in a pod, which made for a bit of head-butting when Glen reached his teens."

"I'll bet."

"Glen wasn't a bad boy. He worked extra-hard to please his father, but things became so strained between them that Glen went off and joined the military right out of high school."

Brady observed the pain in her eyes as she spoke.

"Being in the Marines was good for Glen," Abbey continued. "But in some ways it only seemed to harden him more than before. When he came back, he and his father barely spoke. Glen married his wife, Mary, and took a coaching job at a high school in Southern California. We rarely saw him after that."

"Then Brianna was born," Brady added.

"Yes, she was their firstborn." Abbey's face lit in a smile. "I flew out to L.A. to spend a week with Glen and Mary when Bree came. She was a precious little thing." Abbey's eyes clouded over. "But I could tell Glen wouldn't make the best father, even then. He was so disconnected and"—she paused before she whispered the word—"uncaring. He wasn't the sort to gather a child in his arms and kiss away the tears, if you know what I mean. He was always more interested in whatever team he happened to be coaching than in his own family. Broke my heart."

Brady had to stretch his imagination to understand a man like that. His own father had always bent over backward to show love and compassion, even when Brady hadn't deserved it. Why did Brianna, beautiful girl that she was, have to grow up in a household with such a distant father? Some things just didn't make sense.

"I guess Bree was in sixth grade, maybe seventh, when her little brother, Kyle, was born," Abbey explained. "Kyle's always had a heart of gold."

"Ah." Another interesting twist. If only his own brother had a heart of gold instead of a heart of stone, maybe they'd get along better, have an actual relationship instead of strained conversations.

Abbey paused, and her eyes filled with tears. "That next year, when Bree was just fourteen, something awful happened." She shook her head. "One morning my husband, Norman, wouldn't wake up. I tried and tried to wake him, but"—tears slipped down her wrinkled cheeks, and she didn't even bother to brush them away—"there was nothing I could do."

"I'm so sorry, Abbey," Brady said softly. He knew what it felt like to lose a loved one.

"Doctors said it was an aneurysm. He passed away in his sleep," she whispered. "I guess I should be grateful he didn't suffer. That would be the Christian thing, wouldn't it? To be happy Norman was in the arms of his Maker, safe and sound? That he hadn't struggled in his last few days, like so many?"

Brady nodded but didn't know what to say.

"I had to call Glen and tell him what had happened," Abbey continued. "I knew he'd just been transferred to a new school that fall, a new team, and I didn't know how he would respond. But I wasn't prepared for him to say his team had made it to the play-offs, and he wouldn't be able to come at all."

"Oh, Abbey." He gave her hand a squeeze.

"I—I—had to plan Norman's funeral by myself. There was no one to help me. Just a couple of the ladies from my little church, God bless them, and Pastor Meyers, of course. At the last minute Bree showed up with her mother and Kyle. They were wonderful. But I missed my son. I *needed* my son."

Whoa. What an opposite picture to what his mother had faced. People had swept in around her on every side.

Abbey gazed up into his eyes. "Then"—she started to smile—"a miracle happened."

"A miracle?"

"Bree." Her face came alive as she mentioned her granddaughter's name. "I fell in love with her during that visit, and vice versa. I told her about the university here, and she agreed to look into it when the time came. All those years I prayed, and when she graduated from high school I got the word—she was coming to Pittsburgh! I can tell you there was never a happier day in my life than the day that beautiful girl came marching into my house."

"I can imagine." It all made sense now, why Brianna took such good care of her grandmother, and Abbey of her granddaughter. They had needed one another pretty desperately back then. And now.

"I felt bad for little Kyle back at home. I knew he'd probably not get much fathering. Still, there was little I could do but pray." She shook her head. "But that's a story for another day. I think I've worn out your ears already."

"No, of course not. I wish I had time for more."

Just then Brady's cell phone rang. He looked down at it, fear kicking in. So much for the No Cell Phones hospital policy. "I forgot to turn this off. Sorry." He quickly shut it off.

"Didn't you need to take that call?" Abbey asked.

He shrugged. "It was just my agent. I'll call him back when I get to the car."

"Your agent?"

"Yeah." Brady glanced down at his watch, startled to see the time: 12:20. "I hate to tell you this," he said with a sigh.

"But I have to leave now. I wish I could wait till Brianna gets back, but I just can't."

"Are you going to turn into a pumpkin if you don't leave by a certain time?" Abbey asked.

"I guess you could say that." He stood and pushed his chair back to its original place near the window.

"Wait." Abbey extended her hand. "I know you're in a hurry, but do you have just a minute to pray with me before you go? I'd feel so much better if you would."

"Of course." He walked to the side of the bed and, with love framing every word, began to pray.

❧

Brianna stood at the door of the room, overhearing yet another conversation between her grandmother and Brady. Funny, this one—the tail end of it anyway—seemed to be about her father.

Ironic, considering the fact that she'd spent the last fifteen minutes on the phone with him, begging him to come to Pittsburgh ahead of schedule. To see his mother right away.

He'd argued, of course. The start of the new season and all. Nothing unfamiliar about that story. But by the end of the call she'd convinced him at least to consider the possibility.

"You don't know how long she'll be with us, Dad."

Had she really said those words aloud?

Now, as she stood at the door of her grandmother's room, eavesdropping, she saw the picture from Gran-Gran's point of view. How sad she sounded and how much she needed and wanted her son to be a part of her life.

Determination took over, and Brianna settled the issue in her heart. If her father wouldn't do the right thing, she would. His lack simply made her want to do more. She would pour out love and affection on Gran-Gran at every available opportunity. What was it the Bible said? "But encourage one another daily, as long as it is called Today."

Yes, she would continue to pour herself out on her grand-mother's behalf.

Even if it meant putting off things at work. She would call her boss and ask for vacation time for the next couple of weeks. Whatever it took to keep Gran-Gran's spirits up.

Just then the sound of Brady's voice raised in prayer distracted her. What a great guy he'd turned out to be—in no way like the man she'd first pictured. As she listened in, he prayed for Abbey's healing and then started praying for her family—every member. Brianna wondered at the depth of his words. This was clearly a man familiar with spending time on his knees.

As he finished, she pushed open the door to the room and slipped inside. "Sorry, I didn't mean to interrupt you," she whispered.

"No, it's okay." He flashed her an inviting smile. "We were just wrapping up. I have to leave."

"Do you?" She gave an exaggerated pout, and he laughed.

"I do, but I'll try to come back by later tonight, if you like."

"*I* like." Gran-Gran smiled. "And while you're at it, why don't you stop off at the store and pick up a deck of cards so I can play solitaire?"

"I'm sure they sell cards in the gift shop," Brianna said. She looked at Brady. "So don't you worry about that."

"Well, I'm happy to do it," he said. "But don't count on solitaire. I'll pick up a couple of decks, and we can play hearts. How does that sound?"

"Heavenly!"

Brianna chuckled. Gran-Gran had this guy eating out of her hand. Then again. . .she looked at Brady. He didn't seem to mind a bit. In fact, he appeared to want a reason to return.

He said his good-byes and slipped out of the room, leaving

Brianna alone with her grandmother. She pulled a chair close to the bed and sat.

"I, uh. . .I heard what you said."

"You did? Which part?"

"The part about Dad. All of it."

"Ah." Gran-Gran's cheeks reddened. "I sure didn't mean for you to hear all of that—an old woman rambling about her regrets."

"But you were willing to tell Brady."

"That's different."

"Oh?"

"I guess I should have talked to you about all this stuff years ago," Gran-Gran said with a shrug. "But I know you can't control what your father does any more than I can. I just know"—her lip started to quiver—"that when you get to be my age, you wish you could do a few things over."

Brianna tried to swallow the lump in her throat and nodded. She decided a change of subject was in order. "Well," she said with a smile, "looks like you didn't mind pouring out your heart to our handsome neighbor. If I didn't know any better, I'd say you have a crush on him."

"What?" Her grandmother appeared stunned. "That's just plain silly. But"—she gave Brianna an inquisitive look—"I wouldn't say it's out of the question for *you* to have a crush on him by now."

"M–me? I hardly know the man."

"But what you see you like, right?"

"Gran-Gran, don't."

Her grandmother leaned back and rested her head on the pillows. "I'm just saying, the Lord clearly brought him to Pittsburgh for a reason, and maybe that reason—at least in part—is you."

Brianna stood and began to fuss with her grandmother's

covers, straightening them. "That's just silly. I have no idea why he moved to Pittsburgh, but I'm sure it wasn't to meet a woman. Likely it was business related."

"Maybe. And I have some idea of what business he's in, thanks to a little slip on his part today." Her grandmother's eyes glistened as they always did when she had a secret aching to be shared.

"Oh? What's that?" Brianna asked.

"I think he's an actor," Gran-Gran said with a nod.

"An actor?"

"Yes. You said you overheard our conversation. Did you miss the part where he said his agent called?"

Brianna thought about that a moment. "Yeah, I heard. Guess it slipped right by me." She paused to think about it. "But it doesn't make sense. If he's an actor, what's he doing in Pittsburgh? Why isn't he in L.A. or New York?"

"I don't know, but I'm sure we'll find out. Maybe he's filming a movie here or something. I wouldn't be a bit surprised to find out it was something like that." A few seconds later Gran-Gran's eyelids fluttered shut, and Brianna realized the medication had kicked in.

"Pleasant dreams," she whispered.

"Mm-hmm."

Brianna walked over to the window and looked down onto the parking garage. Somewhere down there Brady was getting into his car and heading off to. . .who knew where?

Funny. She hadn't given much thought to what he did or why he'd come to Pittsburgh. Maybe it didn't matter.

Maybe she was just supposed to settle back and enjoy the fact that he had arrived.

eleven

Brady stopped off at the house, changed clothes, then rode in the back of a plush limousine to the stadium. He arrived with nearly an hour to spare. As he made his way to the media room, he found himself distracted, pondering the fact that he would soon be playing ball right here in this very place. The thing he had hoped and prayed for for years had come to pass. In spite of his past fumbles.

"There's our star player." Burroughs looked over with a nod as he came through the door. "Glad you could join us."

Brady gave him an I'm-sorry smile. "Yeah. Thanks so much for yesterday. I'm really sorry."

"How's the lady? The one who took the fall?"

"My neighbor? Abbey? Her hip was broken, but the doctors pinned her back together," he explained. "I was at the hospital till late last night with her, uh, family."

"*That* story will go to print in a few days," Burroughs said. "STAR QUARTERBACK RUSHES IN TO SAVE THE DAY FOR LOCAL WOMAN. We'll go on to tell them how much you love Pittsburgh, so much so that you'd stop the clock to care for a neighbor in need."

"I, uh, I really don't think that's necessary, sir."

"Why not?" Burroughs slapped him on the back. "It'll make for a good story, and a good story translates into ticket sales. Not hard to figure that one out. We play up every opportunity we can get."

"Hmm." Brady wasn't sure how Abbey would react if she read her name in the paper. Or Brianna. He shuddered, thinking about it. What would she say? Would she feel taken advantage of?

He would find some way to smooth this over. Or talk Burroughs out of leaking the story.

Coach Carter entered the room with a jersey in his hands, which he tossed to Brady. "You've got your work cut out for you between now and tomorrow night. Hope your memorization skills are as good as your plays."

"Thanks." Brady slipped on the jersey, loving the way it felt.

Minutes later a stocky man with a thick mustache entered the room. Brady stood at once. "Mr. Mandel." He extended his hand toward the team's owner, who shook it with vigor.

"Glad to meet you, son." Mandel patted Brady on the back. "We're counting on you to pull us out of a slump."

"Yes, sir. I'll give it my best shot."

"I know you will."

Brady swallowed hard and sat back down, and the room slowly filled with reporters, no doubt armed and ready to snag their story.

At three o'clock straight up, Burroughs approached the microphone with Mandel at his side. Brady watched it all, his excitement building. The reporters—who till now had been talking loudly among themselves and snapping an occasional photograph—grew silent. The clicking of cameras filled the room.

"Thank you all for coming," Mandel said with a nod. "The news today is good. As you know, Harper's out of the game. That left us with a hole in our line. We've had our feelers out, and I'm proud to announce today that Pittsburgh has a new starting quarterback, Brady Campbell."

He motioned to Brady, who smiled broadly. At once the cameras shifted his way. He nodded.

Mandel continued on with a look of confidence. "Brady is more than going to fill Harper's shoes, starting tomorrow night. We're looking forward to our best season ever."

The reporters tried to toss out a couple of questions, but Burroughs interrupted them. "Coach Carter will speak for a few minutes, and then you can ask your questions."

Carter stood and approached the podium. He started a rapid-fire dissertation of Brady's skills, homing in on his successes in Tampa over the past two years. Afterward he gestured for Brady to join him at the microphone.

Brady trembled as he opened his mouth to speak. "First, let me say how excited I am to be here. I had two great years in Tampa. Great years. Got my start in the league there. For a while it looked as if I might be watching the game from the sofa this year. But coming here to Pittsburgh, to be part of this franchise, is a dream come true for me. To lead this football team is"—he stumbled over the words as the lump in his throat made it difficult to speak—"to lead this team is nothing short of a miracle."

Mandel slipped into the spot behind him and put his arm over his shoulders. "You know how I feel, folks. Winning is about growing. Getting better. We're committed to getting better, and adding Campbell to our family of players does just that—makes the whole team better. I truly believe this is going to be the best year ever for our fans." At this point Mandel opened the floor to questions.

"How are you adjusting to life without beaches?" one reporter asked.

Brady laughed. "That's an easy one. I didn't get to the beach much. The field was my beach."

"Yeah, but you know it snows here," another reporter added. "Even on the field." They all erupted in laughter, obviously aimed at Brady.

"That's what I hear."

"Have you ever played in snow before, Campbell?" the reporter asked with a smirk. "For that matter, have you ever *seen* snow before?"

"Seen it." Brady looked at the coach for reassurance before admitting. "Played on it a couple of times over the years." He tried to think of something clever. A smile rose to his lips. "But I plan to move so fast that it melts underneath me, so I doubt it will be a problem."

Another round of laughter rang out, this time in his support.

"Why didn't Tampa renew your contract this season?" one reporter asked.

Brady cleared his throat, then spoke with as much confidence as he could muster. "I leave the negotiations to my agent, and he leaves the passing and throwing to me."

"Any reason why you weren't picked up by another team?" another reporter called out.

Brady shrugged. "Just wasn't God's plan, I guess."

"God?" A couple of the guys chuckled. "So are you saying God led you here—to Pittsburgh?"

Brady noticed the look of surprise in Burroughs's eyes but forged ahead. "Well, I guess you could put it that way."

"He's here now, and that's what matters," Burroughs interjected. "And we're happy to have him. We know the fans will be, too."

"Especially the women!" one reporter threw in. "Are you still a ladies' man, Campbell?"

Brady felt his cheeks flush and simply shrugged to avoid the dreaded subject. *Lord, please don't let this story go any further.*

"I'm not the man I was back in Tampa; let's just leave it at that."

The time came to pose for a few photos. Brady put on

a winning smile and stood alongside his new coach and manager. With the cameras in his face and the jersey on his back, he was ready—ready to run for the goal.

❧

Brianna thought back to her last bit of time at the hospital as she pulled away in her car. At ten minutes till three Gran-Gran had announced her need to watch the news conference, which gave Brianna the perfect opportunity to slip away for a couple of hours.

"I have some grocery shopping to do," she said. "But I'll be back later tonight if that's okay with you."

"Of course, of course!" Her grandmother had waved her away, turning to the television, and Brianna slipped out the door, content for some time alone to plan for the days ahead.

Now, as she made her way north, she found her thoughts drifting to Brady. Despite her earlier thoughts, Gran-Gran was right. What she saw she liked. A lot.

But did he like her, too? Would it be presumptuous to think so after such a short time? Interesting to think about it.

On the other hand, she needed to shake off this childish fantasy and stay focused on her grandmother. She would have plenty of time in the future for romance. Right now Gran-Gran needed her, and she came first.

Brianna whipped the car into the parking lot of the grocery store and got busy making her purchases. By the time her grandmother returned home in a few weeks, Brianna would be ready with some of her favorite foods. She would spend the weeks learning.

And Brady.

Maybe she would invite him over for dinner. Let him know she had acquired at least a bit of her grandmother's talent in the kitchen.

Brianna left the grocery store with a smile on her face.

Once she got home and put the groceries away, she would rest a few minutes then head back up to the hospital.

Hmm. Maybe she'd better call Gran-Gran before leaving the house, just in case she wanted or needed anything from home.

Lost in her thoughts, Brianna made her way toward the duplex. When she pulled onto the street, she almost didn't recognize it as her own. A mob of television vans lined each side, as well as cars and vans bearing the logos of prominent radio stations. They seemed to be centered in front of her house.

Or were they? How could she tell through the traffic?

She honked at a fellow with a television camera in his hand as she attempted to pull her car into the driveway. *What?* He pointed the camera in her direction, and for a moment she wanted to jump out of her car and smack the guy. He had some nerve!

With her pulse racing, she drove slowly up the driveway toward the garage. The second she stepped out of the car, a mob of reporters surrounded her on every side, many of them shoving cameras in her face. She couldn't make heads or tails out of what they were saying.

At first.

But then one name rang through, clear as a bell: Brady Campbell.

"B–Brady?" she stammered. "W–what about him?"

A female reporter who introduced herself as a sportscaster for a cable affiliate started a round of questioning. "Can you confirm that Brady Campbell lives next door? If so, can you tell us anything about him?"

"Well, I, uh, he's a great guy," Brianna managed to say. "But why do you want to know?"

A laugh went up from the crowd. "Why do we want to

know?" One male reporter jeered. "That's priceless."

"So tell me," the female reporter continued, "how does it feel living next door to the man who's going to take our team to the Super Bowl this year?"

"What?" For a minute there Brianna thought the woman said Super Bowl.

"We hear Brady was quite a ladies' man back in Florida," another reporter threw out. "A woman on each arm and a party that never ended."

A woman on each arm? Parties? They had to have the wrong guy. Surely.

"Would you say Pittsburgh has changed him much?" the female reporter asked. "Or are old habits hard to break?"

"Yeah, is he throwing any passes your way?" another man hollered out.

A roar of laughter went up from the crowd, and Brianna turned to face the man, anger rising to the surface. Enough was enough.

"Look," she said. "I don't know what you're talking about— any of you—but this much I do know. You're trespassing on private property. You are going to get off my lawn, or I'll call the police and have you removed."

Several of them backed off right away, and a few of the ones who remained gave her the oddest looks she'd ever seen. As if she'd just spoken to them in a foreign language.

"Lady, are you kidding?" one asked.

"We thought you'd be thrilled to tell us about Brady," someone else said with a shrug. "No harm intended."

He and the others trekked across the lawn to Brady's drive-way, where one or two began to photograph and videotape his side of the duplex. Brianna stood in stunned silence as she attempted to figure out what had just transpired.

She raced back through the tidbits of conversation in an

attempt to make sense of things. Surely the woman hadn't said Super Bowl? Brady was an actor, right?

An idea began to emerge, one she couldn't shake. Maybe the paparazzi had followed him here. Maybe all that stuff about women and parties was part of a gag, something his agent had cooked up to draw publicity for a movie or something.

Still. . . Even at that, something about all this just felt wrong.

Brianna grabbed her bags of groceries and shot inside the house, ignoring her phone, which was ringing nonstop. Once inside the safety of the kitchen, she looked down to discover she'd missed three calls.

From Gran-Gran.

She called back right away, amazed at the emotion in her grandmother's voice as she cried out, "Bree!"

"Y—yes?"

"You're not going to believe it!" Gran-Gran let out a squeal. "Brady Campbell—the one and only Brady Campbell—*our* Brady Campbell—"

"Y—yes?"

"He's our new quarterback!" Her grandmother began an animated conversation about all she had seen and heard during the press conference, but Brianna never heard a word. Everything was starting to spin out of control.

Was it possible? Could it be? Mr. Trouble with a capital T was just that—trouble. Only a different kind from what she'd expected.

With Gran-Gran still chattering away, Brianna snuck a peek out of the kitchen window, staring in horrified awe at the crowd of people on Brady's lawn. The news teams clearly wanted to meet him face-to-face—drill him full of questions about his past and his future.

A wave of nausea came over Brianna, and she dropped

down into a chair. Her hands trembled as the grim reality set in. She'd done it again—fallen for a guy whose first love was the game. Only one problem this time. . .

This guy didn't *love* football.

This guy *was* football.

twelve

After the press conference Brady decided to swing back by the house to send a few e-mails before going to the hospital. He arrived home to an unexpected mob scene. As the limo driver eased the car down the road, the press met them on every side. They started pounding on his car windows before he ever hit the driveway, shouting questions at him through the tinted glass.

You've got to be kidding me.

The driver managed to pull up to the curb, and Brady mumbled a thank-you, then wrangled his way out of the backseat, hands up in the air. "Easy, fellas!" he said, as one guy almost hit him in the head with a microphone on an extended boom stand. "I'd like to live to play my first game if you don't mind."

They began to barrage him with questions, many of which he was able to answer without trouble. He only stumbled when they got to the part about his last year in Tampa.

"So you spent some time in a twelve-step program," one of them jabbed. "What was that like? Are you clean and sober now?"

"I, um. . ." He raked his fingers through his hair, embarrassed, yet knowing this was a question he couldn't avoid. "I haven't touched a drink in months. In fact, my whole life has changed—every aspect of it."

"Would you like to elaborate?" a female reporter asked.

"I–I'm a different man. I'm not the old Brady Campbell anymore. I'm the new, improved version."

"Same throwing arm?" one of the guys jeered.

"Yeah, same arm. Just different. . .heart."

On and on they went, pounding him with questions and asking about his new team members. And the one who'd preceded him.

"What's your opinion of Harper?" the female reporter asked. "Do you feel like you can fill his shoes?"

"Harper's great," Brady acknowledged. "One of the best players in the game today. I wish him the best with his recovery, and I'm honored to take up where he left off. But I am *not* Harper. I'm Brady Campbell. So don't look for me to lead the team in exactly the same way, okay?"

Just then something caught Brady's eye. Brianna, in the next driveway, slipping into her car. She glanced his way with an odd look. He could read the pain in her eyes, but why? What was up with that?

Ah. She was probably a little confused. He hadn't exactly prepared her for this, had he? Then again he couldn't have. Keeping everything under wraps had been critical. But now he could tell her everything. And she would not only understand, but he hoped she would also celebrate alongside him, as would Abbey.

If he could just get to her through this crowd.

Brady managed to shake off the reporters, promising to give them all interviews at a later date. As they dispersed, he watched Brianna pull away. He wanted to run after her, but she seemed intent on leaving.

Well, no problem. He would catch up with her later. . .at the hospital. Surely by then the frenzy would be behind him.

He hoped.

❧

Brianna pulled up a chair next to her grandmother's bed and did her best to ignore the zeal in the reporter's voice from the television across the room.

"Listen, Bree—they're talking about Brady again."

"Uh-huh." She refused to look. Let them talk. Why should she care?

"Well, listen to this—why don't you—?"

The reporter's interview covered Brady's past plays on the field and off. In a clip at the end Brady added a few lines, insisting he wasn't the man he used to be.

Whatever.

As the report came to an end, Brianna turned toward her grandmother, who couldn't seem to say enough about Brady.

"I just knew there was something special about that boy. I knew it."

"But you heard what those reporters said," Brianna argued. "He's got a—a past."

Gran-Gran gave her a scrutinizing look. "We've all got a past, Bree. That's why we need Christ so much."

"Well, I know, but this is different. He's going around talking like he's a Christian, and then every news channel flashes photos of him in bars. With women."

"But you heard what he said in that last interview," her grandmother scolded. "He said he's a different man now. His heart is different. And you know what that means. You've spent time with him. It's clear to see that his sins have been washed away—just like yours—just like mine."

Brianna let out a lingering sigh. "Well, if it's true he's a different man, and I'm not so sure it is, then he should have warned us about this football thing. Should have told us why he'd come to town in the first place."

"Why? Why should he have told us?"

"Well, I don't know. He just should have. It would've been polite."

"Bree, I don't expect you to understand this," Gran-Gran

said in a sympathetic voice. "But I'm sure they had him under a gag order. He couldn't breathe a word. But now that this press conference is behind him, I'd imagine he'll show up ready to talk. And when he does—"

At that exact moment a rap on the door interrupted her grandmother's sentence. Brianna looked across the room, startled to see Brady standing there with a fistful of pink roses. Tea roses, no less. Her grandmother's favorite.

"For the lady of honor," Brady said as he took a step in their direction.

Brianna wasn't sure whose hand he was going to place the roses in. Just in case, she turned her head and shifted her gaze out the window. *I will not, under any circumstances, let that man think I would expect—or even take—those flowers from him.*

She turned back in time to see him pass the roses to Gran-Gran, who took them with a squeal.

"You're the best, Brady." She gestured for him to sit— which he did upon her command—then gave him a motherly look. "But as tickled as I am, I still think you need a good spanking."

Brady's gaze shifted to the floor. "Yeah, I'm really sorry, but I couldn't say anything. They wouldn't let me."

"See, Bree. I *told* you!" Gran-Gran crossed her arms in front of her, as if that settled the whole thing. Brianna shrugged, as though it didn't matter. But what she really wanted to do was give Mr. Campbell a piece of her mind.

She glanced at her watch then bounded from her chair. "I, um, I really need to leave."

"Leave?" Gran-Gran and Brady spoke in unison.

"Um, yeah. I'm really tired. Didn't get much sleep last night. And I'm kind of hungry, too."

"Well, let me take you to get some food." Brady rose to his feet.

"I really think I just need some rest," she explained. "So if you don't mind. . ." She made her way to the edge of the bed and gave Gran-Gran a kiss on the cheek. "By the way," she said, "I called Pastor Meyers early this morning before the service started. Apologized for not being there and told him why. He and his wife are coming by to see you later this evening."

"Well, bless you for that. And bless them, too."

Brianna nodded and turned to leave. As she did, she noticed the pleading look in Brady's eyes.

Well, let him plead. She didn't feel like talking right now.

Maybe another day.

thirteen

Brady looked at Abbey, stunned. "What's up with that? She's not speaking to me?"

"I guess not."

"Because I didn't tell her who I was?" he asked. "Is that it, or is there more to it?"

A look of pain crossed Abbey's face as she shifted her position in the bed. "There's more to it than that. I know this might not make much sense, but Bree is a little sensitive about football."

"Football *players*, or the game in general?"

"The game in general. It all goes back to something that happened with her father when she was in high school, but I'm not the one to tell that tale," Abbey said. "Besides, I think it will do Bree good to get it off her chest." She added, "I have a feeling you might be just the one to win her over."

"To the sport?" he asked.

With a twinkle in her eyes Abbey answered, "Among other things."

"Humph. That would require her actually staying in the same room with me for more than five seconds."

"She will," Abbey said with a nod. "I know that girl better than I know myself." Her eyes lit up. "So why don't you go after her?"

Brady shook his head, confused. "I don't even know where she's going."

"Oh, I do. Every time she gets frustrated, she goes to the same place. I'll be happy to give you directions." She pointed to the tablet and pen on her bedside table, and Brady scribbled down the details.

"Are you sure?" he asked.

"Sure as I'm living and breathing." Abbey clamped her hand over her mouth as soon as the words escaped. "Maybe I should've phrased that another way." She gave him a wink to let him know she was teasing.

Brady said good-bye and turned to leave. Just as he reached the door, Abbey called to him. "Hey, Brady?"

"Yes?" He faced her.

More wrinkles than usual etched her brow as she whispered, "Ask her about Daniel."

Brady paused then shrugged. "Okay."

Just as he attempted to walk through the door, two elderly women met him head-on. They took one look at him, and exaggerated squealing began.

"Hush, ladies," Abbey insisted. "Or the nurse will toss you out on your ears!"

After a minute or so of whispered glee, one of them appeared to hyperventilate. Her red-orange curls bounced up and down as she tried to catch her breath. For a second Brady wasn't sure if she was *really* struggling to breathe or simply acting.

Yep. Acting.

The woman extended her hand with a sly grin and introduced herself. "I'm Lora Patterson," she said, "and you're— you're—Brady Campbell."

"Yes. Good to meet you."

He extended his hand, and she took it but refused to let go. When he finally managed to break free, she clutched her hand to her chest with a dreamy-eyed look on her face. "I'm never washing this hand as long as I live!"

From the bed Abbey let out a grunt. "Then don't count on

coming back to my house for dinner."

"Oh, hush, Abbey." Lora's cheeks flushed as she made her way to the side of the bed. "Let me have some fun."

"Well, that's a fine how-do-you-do after all I've been through," Abbey said with a pout.

Brady wanted to slip out before they engaged him in conversation, but the woman left standing in the doorway was, well, a bit on the wide side. And she didn't appear to be moving anytime soon. Instead she stared at him in bug-eyed silence with her mouth hanging open.

"Move out of the way, Rena," Abbey scolded. "Brady was just leaving."

"D–do you have to?" The woman looked as if she might cry.

"I'm sorry, but I was just—"

"He's going after *Bree*," Abbey explained. "So scoot, Rena. Let the man pass."

"B–but I wanted to ask for his autograph," Rena stammered. She reached into her purse and came up with a grocery store receipt and an ink pen. "Sorry, but it's the best I can do," she said as she shoved them both in Brady's direction.

He gave her a warm smile and quickly scribbled his name.

"How ironic is that!" she said, as she pointed to the paper. "You signed your name right on top of the word *honey*."

Abbey rolled her eyes. "Rena, stop flirting."

"I'm not flirting." The woman batted her eyelashes and gave a girlish giggle.

"Excuse her, Brady," Lora said. "She doesn't get out much."

"Yeah," Rena acknowledged with a wistful smile. "My back goes out more than I do."

All three women erupted in laughter. Brady joined in—for a minute. But he couldn't stay there forever. He needed to catch up with Brianna. He nodded in the direction of the women—"Happy to meet you both"—then shot out of the door while the shooting was good.

Minutes later he found himself on the highway, headed toward his destination. What he would say when he got there was a mystery. Still, if he didn't follow her, if he didn't let her know he cared about what she was thinking, feeling...

Hmm.

He *cared* about what she was thinking and feeling.

The revelation hit him hard. How long had it been since he'd cared—*really* cared—about what someone else thought about him? Years probably. Something about sobering up brought back his ability to care. To genuinely care.

And this was a girl worth caring about.

He pulled into the parking lot of the tiny strip mall, just a few blocks from home. Where was it? Ah, yes. On the end. Steel City Scoop-a-Rama—Pittsburgh's premiere ice cream eatery, according to Abbey. And Bree's favorite spot for drowning her sorrows.

Brady entered the store and walked up behind her. He listened with a smile as she ordered a deluxe double scoop of white chocolate mocha with an extra serving of candy bar "mixin's" stirred in. The fellow behind the counter placed the scoops of ice cream on a marble slab and began to mash the bits of crunchy chocolate candy into it. Then he pressed the whole conglomeration into a large waffle cone, also coated in chocolate.

"Sprinkles on top?" he asked.

Brianna leaned her elbows on the countertop and stared at the cone. "Mm-hmm. Yeah. Lots of 'em."

Wow. When this girl drowned her sorrows, she drowned her sorrows. Likely she'd be up all night on a sugar high, if he didn't step in and do something about it.

The clerk handed her the cone and rang up her total. Six dollars and forty-nine cents? That was a high price to pay for an emotional breakdown, even a well-deserved one.

Brady remained behind her, still and silent, as Brianna fumbled around in her purse with her free hand for the money. Her moves grew more frantic. "I—I can't find my wallet."

"Excuse me?" The young clerk gave her a suspicious glare, and she started looking again, nearly tipping the cone over in the process.

"Maybe I left it in the car. Or maybe. . ." She looked at the fellow again, her voice quivering. "I know what I did. I left my wallet at the hospital. I'd taken it out to get some change to buy a soda, and I must've forgotten to put it back in." She stared at the cone as ice cream dribbled down the sides. "What should I do?"

The kid let out an exasperated sigh, then reached out to take the cone from her hand.

And Brady, quiet until now, pulled out his wallet.

❧

Brianna saw the hand reach around from behind her and heard the credit card slap down on the counter. She turned, half horrified and half grateful. When she saw Brady's face, her stomach knotted. What was he doing here?

She shook her head. "I can't let you do that."

"You can and you will," he said. "Because you're going to share it with me. If we can get to it before it melts into a puddle." He reached to take it from her hand, then licked it around the edges.

How gross is that? Brianna let out a groan, more for effect than anything else. "Now you're going to have to eat the whole thing."

"No, I'm not."

Unbelievable.

Then again, he *was* paying for her ice cream. Once again he'd swept in and saved the day. How many times was he going to do that?

The kid behind the counter swiped Brady's card and waited on the machine to respond.

"How did you know I was here?" Brianna asked. Then, knowing the answer in her heart, added a quick, "Never mind. Skip that."

"It was right of her to tell me," Brady answered, taking a nibble from the edge of the cone. "I know you're upset at me, and I want to get to the bottom of it."

She crossed her arms. "I never said I was upset."

"You didn't have to."

The clerk started to hand Brady his credit card. But then he glanced down at the name on the card and back up again into Brady's face.

"Hey, you're Brady Campbell."

"Uh. . .yeah." Brady took the card and shoved it into his wallet then handed the cone to Brianna.

"Our new starting quarterback. From Tampa."

Brianna groaned. Would it always be like this when Brady was around?

"I saw the press conference. My name is Kevin Nelson. I play for North Hills High School."

"That's great," Brady said with a smile.

He gestured to a table across the room, and Brianna, grateful to be away from the kid behind the counter, headed over to it. She sat down and began to lick the edges of the cone to keep the drips from landing in her lap.

In spite of an incoming crowd of teenagers, the kid who'd waited on them seemed intent on staring. Even from across the room she saw him pull out his cell phone. Was he making a call? Brianna tried to ignore him, but he seemed to have the crazy thing pointed straight at them.

She jabbed Brady in the arm. "What is he doing?"

Brady turned around, and the clerk pressed a button on

his cell phone. A camera.

She slapped herself in the head. "I can't take you anywhere."

"Things will simmer down soon. Once the dust settles from the media hype, I'll just be an average Joe."

"Somehow I doubt that."

"Can you tell me why you're suddenly so upset at me? Is it because I didn't tell you who I was?"

A wave of guilt washed over Brianna as she saw the confused look in his eyes. What had he done to her? And yet she must say something; otherwise, he might go on staring her down for the rest of the night.

"I just have an aversion to football—that's all. Long story."

"Is it the thing about your dad being a coach? The stuff you told me earlier?"

"That and a lot more." She shifted in her seat, uncomfortable with the direction of the conversation.

"I'm here if you want to talk."

She wanted to open up, wanted to tell him the whole story. How much she'd loved Daniel. How he'd been the star player on her father's team their senior year in high school. How he'd already received a scholarship to play for UCLA the next year. How her father had destroyed all of that with one thoughtless decision.

"I'll let you know when I'm ready," she said finally.

"I understand." Brady paused then surprised her with his next words. "One reason I wanted to see you was to tell you something. All those news stories about what I was like back in Tampa. . ."

She drew in a deep breath before answering. "Those television reporters didn't paint a very rosy picture of you."

"That was the old me." He gave her an imploring look. "You have to trust me. The old Brady Campbell is dead and gone. Those things I used to do—they felt good for a season.

But that season is over. God has given me a fresh start."

"I understand fresh starts. I do."

"Can I ask you a question?"

She shrugged. "Sure. Go ahead."

"Who is Daniel?"

Brianna nearly choked on her ice cream. "Daniel? How did you know about him?" He opened his mouth to answer, but she stopped him. "Let me guess." *Gran-Gran, this is too much. You shouldn't have opened that door.*

"I'm sorry," he began. "I didn't mean to—"

"Forget it." Just then the kid who'd waited on them drew near to their table, cell phone open wide. What was he up to? "I have to go." Brianna stood, anxious to escape.

"But why? Because of what I said?" Brady reached to touch her arm—a gesture of kindness, she knew—but she shook him off.

"I just need to get away for a while by myself to think."

And with no other explanation than that, she left him sitting at the Steel City Scoop-a-Rama. Alone.

fourteen

As Brady settled down on the sofa to read the local paper early Monday morning, he was horrified to discover the whole saga of how he had helped Abbey on the day of her accident, plastered on the front page. The headline read, QUARTERBACK RIDES INTO TOWN ON WHITE HORSE.

"Oh, no. Please, no."

Surely Mack Burroughs was to blame for this. But why? After a lengthy discussion by phone late Sunday night, Burroughs had promised to do the right thing. Brady assumed that meant *not* running the story.

Then again, maybe Burroughs thought exposure for one of his key players *was* the right thing. Who knew? But, as Brady scanned the article, a sickening feeling came over him.

For the most part, the story had the facts straight. But it made him out to be some kind of superhero. What would Abbey and Brianna do when they read this slanted write-up? Would they come after him with a spatula in hand and run him out of town?

No telling.

Brady tried to put together a plan of action for what he would say to them tomorrow when he made another visit to the hospital, but he couldn't think clearly. Tonight's game— and that intensive playbook—had him preoccupied.

Instinctively Brady flipped to the sports section of the paper for a glance-through before his morning shower. He almost fell off the couch when he came across several photos of him and Brianna, obviously taken by the kid at the Scoop-a-Rama. One showed Brady holding a dripping ice cream cone, licking the edges as Brianna looked on in interest. The caption underneath read, QUARTERBACK MAKES GOOD ON CLAIM TO MELT ICE.

Brady groaned as he noticed another photo—a shot of Brianna with her finger pointed toward him and an angry look on her face. The caption underneath proclaimed, LOCAL WOMAN RESISTS CAMPBELL'S CHARMS. The article went on to tell the whole story of his problems in Tampa. It was all in there—his issues with women and drinking and his claims of recovery. Everything.

Brady laid the paper on the coffee table and leaned his head into his hands. He wanted to pray—wanted to see this remedied—and quickly—but hardly knew where to begin. He was no longer worried about simply offending Brianna. Now he worried that she and Abbey might never speak to him again. How had he managed to drag them into this? And what could he do to undrag them?

He thought about it as he showered and then dressed for the day. He pondered it as he drove to the practice. He prayed about it as he geared up for the game. And he agonized over it as the lights on the field came alive, revealing thousands upon thousands of screaming fans.

If he could just get through tonight's game. . .he would make everything okay again.

Somehow.

◦•

Brianna paced the hallway of the hospital, avoiding her grandmother's room at all costs. Inside Rena and Lora sat on either side of the bed, waving their pennants as always and shouting craziness to the television.

"Use your hospital voices, ladies!" Brianna had encouraged them. Not that it appeared to matter. Folks in nearly every room seemed to be watching the game, and a rousing cheer went up from the whole floor as Brady led the team to victory.

The whole thing proved to be more than irritating; it was downright annoying, particularly in light of today's events.

She fumed as she went back over the newspaper articles in her mind. How could Brady have used the incident with her grandmother to promote himself? Did he not realize Gran-Gran would be hurt?

Okay, so she wasn't really hurt. And, yes, she'd actually enjoyed the story, claiming it cemented her as the Steelers' biggest fan. But, really, what right did Brady have to tell the press about her grandmother in the first place? Would he do anything to get a story, even at the expense of others?

She continued to pace long after the game ended. Finally, when she could wait no longer, Brianna made her way back into the room and pretended to busy herself with a magazine.

"Brady Campbell is the best thing that ever happened to us," Gran-Gran declared with a satisfied look on her face. "Handsome—and a great player to boot! And he got me my first-ever write-up in the paper. Eighty-four years I've lived and have never seen my name in the paper once. Till now. Gotta give the boy a hand for that and for leading us to victory tonight!"

At that she let out a whoop, and the other ladies followed suit. Brianna rolled her eyes. Obviously they didn't see Brady as a problem.

Hmm. If they didn't, why did she?

Well, never mind all that right now. She needed to shoo her grandmother's visitors out of the room. She did so with the wave of a hand.

"Ladies, I think it's time for Gran-Gran to get her beauty sleep. Doctor's orders."

"Aw, do they hafta leave?" her grandmother asked with a pout. "I'm in the mood for a slumber party."

"No sleepovers tonight," Brianna scolded.

Lora stood, and Rena tried to follow suit. She let out an exaggerated groan as she finally made her way to her feet, followed by a winsome, "If I'd known I was gonna live this long, I would've taken better care of myself."

After a bit more grumbling, the two older women headed out of the room, singing Brady's praises all the way. They waved their good-byes at the door but never stopped the chatter for a minute.

Gran-Gran settled back against the pillow and yawned. "You missed a great game, Bree," she said. "You have no idea how good Brady is."

"It's more likely we have no idea how *bad* he is," she muttered in response.

"Careful now, girl," Gran-Gran said with a frown. She turned back to the television. "Oh, look—the news is on!" She reached for the remote to turn up the sound. The television reporter was giving an animated play-by-play of the game. From the background clips Brianna could see Brady truly was a great player, maybe better than most she'd seen. But that didn't make him a good person, did it?

The story ended, and she'd just reached down to give Gran-Gran a good-night kiss on the cheek when the lead for an upcoming story grabbed her attention. What was that the news reporter said? Something about Brady and an ice-cream video?

She turned to face the television, her jaw dropping as she watched a rough, unedited video clip. *Oh, no!*

It was all there, the two of them seated together at the Steel City Scoop-a-Rama, talking. Brady taking her by the arm when she tried to leave. Oh, dear. How did that crazy kid videotape this? Was that even possible on a cell phone?

As the news clip ended, her grandmother gave her an inquisitive look, then spoke softly. "It was obvious he didn't want you to leave. He wanted you to stay with him."

"I guess." She exhaled a sigh as she replayed the look on Brady's face over and over again. Maybe he *hadn't* wanted her to leave, but that hadn't stopped her, had it?

"Are you sure you can't give him one more chance, honey?" Gran-Gran reached over and stroked her arm. "He's a great guy."

Brianna shrugged and reached for her purse. "I'll pray about it," she promised. "That's about all I can offer at this point."

"Well, then!" Her grandmother's smile lit the room. "Don't be surprised if the Lord grabs hold of that prayer and does something with it, something remarkable."

"Trust me—nothing would surprise me at this point." Brianna kissed Gran-Gran on the cheek once more and headed for the door. She stopped just as she reached it and turned back. "But answer this one question for me."

"Yes?"

"Are you gonna go on matchmaking forever?"

A serious look came over her grandmother's face before she answered. "Well, on *this* side of forever anyway. Don't likely know as I'll go on doing it from the *other* side." She gave Bree a playful wink.

"You're a pill. You know that?"

"Yeah, I know," Gran-Gran said as she fussed with the sheets. "But you love me."

"More than life itself." Brianna blew her grandmother a kiss and headed off on her way home.

fifteen

Brady spent the next few weeks fending off reporters and practicing with the team. A cool front hovered over Pittsburgh, and it seemed to have affected Brianna's heart. He'd noticed it nearly every time he visited with Abbey at the hospital and then the rehab facility, but that hadn't kept him from trying. A couple of times he'd gone knocking at Brianna's door, thinking she was holed up inside the house. Not once had she answered the door.

One Friday morning, as he sat reading the paper, Brady noticed some movement through the open blinds at his living room window. He eased his way toward it and watched Brianna pull her car into the driveway next door. So Abbey was home at last. He would rest much easier knowing that.

He headed out the front door right away with a smile on his face, ready to be of assistance. He made it over to Brianna's car in seconds and helped her pull the walker from the trunk. She nodded her appreciation. Then he went to the passenger side and opened the front door for Abbey.

"Glad you're home!" he said with a wink as he extended his hand.

With his help she managed to stand. Then, with Brianna's support, Abbey gripped the walker and took a couple of steps.

"Would you mind getting those?" Brianna gestured to two small suitcases and a plastic bag with the hospital's name on it.

"I'd be happy to." Brady walked along behind them until they reached the front porch. Once there Brianna handed him the house key, and he opened the aging wooden door with a grin. "Welcome home!"

He followed the ladies into the living room, startled to see a twin bed where the love seat used to sit. Abbey made her way over to it with a look of chagrin on her face.

Brady gave Brianna an inquisitive look.

"Had to," she whispered. "Doctor's orders."

"I might be old, but I'm not deaf," Abbey interjected. "Besides, you won't hurt my feelings by speaking up. I'm not ready to climb those stairs just yet. Not for another week or so."

"How did you get the bed down here?" he asked Brianna.

"Pastor Meyers helped," she said with a shrug. "We put the love seat in the garage for now. It's just temporary."

A sense of disappointment came over Brady as he realized Brianna hadn't come to him for help.

Brianna helped her grandmother get situated in the bed, and Brady made himself busy putting the walker in the front hall closet. He looked around the room again, stunned at how different it looked. It's hospital-like decor made him a little uncomfortable.

"Gran-Gran, I need to get your prescriptions filled," Brianna said, reaching for her purse.

"Would you like for me to sit with her while you're gone?" Brady offered.

"You, um, don't mind?"

"No. Not at all."

After Brianna left, Abbey gave Brady a woeful shrug. "Kind of sad that I need a sitter, don't you think?"

"Of course not! I'm just a friend here for a visit. That's all."

She sighed as she looked around the room. "I don't think I'm going to enjoy sleeping in here; that's sure and certain. The sun comes in through that window in the morning."

Her brow wrinkled in concern. "But I guess I'll manage, regardless. It's only for a week or so."

"Well, you do as the doctor says," Brady encouraged her. "No stair climbing until he says it's okay. Don't go trying to be a hero."

"No, *you're* the hero," she said. "You're the best player we've seen in years. I've been watching you, you know."

"Hardly the best." He paused then gave a more detailed apology than the one he'd given her at the hospital for the ongoing news stories, along with a lengthy description of what had really happened, including the part about his troubles back in Florida. He ended by telling her about his conversion to Christ, focusing on the role his mother had played in leading him to the Lord.

"She sounds like someone I would like," Abbey said.

"Oh, you'd love her." He paused then said, "And I know she knows I'm solid in my relationship with the Lord, so I'm not sure why I worry so much about what other people think. I guess, because I'm in the limelight, I just want to be careful—I don't want to give God a bad name." He let out an exaggerated sigh.

"You're worried for nothing, Brady," Abbey said. "When I watch those news stories, all I see is a man who's no longer what he used to be. A man who wants a second chance. Just like all of us at one point or another."

"Thank you." He smiled.

"And besides," she added, "there's hardly a person mentioned in the Bible who didn't give the Lord a bad name. David was a murderer but went on to be called a man after God's own heart. And Paul, before he came to the Lord, put Christian converts to death. Several of the great men of faith, like Abraham, for example, got ahead of the Lord and created their own plans. Peter, one of Jesus' disciples, denied Him several times over but still went on to do great exploits for Him. Shall I go on?"

"Nah. No point." Brady felt relief wash over him as she spoke. Somehow, talking to Abbey always made things better. She seemed to feel the words, as if she'd lived them personally.

"Good. Now let's talk about Bree," Abbey said, looking rather stern.

"What about her?"

"Well, it's clear to me God has brought you here to Pittsburgh for a reason—other than just playing football, I mean—and I'm convinced it's to marry my granddaughter."

"O–oh?" For a second Brady was stunned. "What makes you so sure?"

"I just know in my knower. And trust me—my knower's been around long enough to get it right much of the time."

"I see. So what do you suggest I do about this?"

"Well, we've lost several weeks, what with me being in the hospital and all. We've got to make up for lost time. First order of business will be to watch and pray. Time will be the thing that wins her over. That and a few more winning games from you."

"Brianna cares about football scores?"

"Well, no. . ." Abbey's gaze shifted, and he noticed a smile. "But a few winning games would continue to win *me* over, and that's very important if you're going to develop a relationship with her."

"Aha. I see. Well, I wouldn't want to lose your favor, that's for sure." He smiled, then looked out the window as he thought about Brianna. It would likely take more than time to win her over. But to start the ball rolling, he had to know more about her.

Some things, of course, were obvious. Clearly she was a strong Christian, vastly different from most of the women he had known. But would a girl who had followed the Lord most of her life give a guy like him a second glance? Did she question his relationship with the Lord? He wouldn't blame her. She only had the news reports to go on, and they appeared to contradict it. But what could he do about that? Seemed a bit futile even to ponder the idea of winning her heart.

And what was up with the football thing? So her dad was into the game. Neglected the family. Was that really enough to keep her from developing a friendship with someone involved in the sport? Maybe this would be a good time to ask the big question.

"I, um, I tried to ask her about Daniel that night at the ice cream shop," he started.

"Oh?"

"She shut me down. I could tell that was a closed door."

"Well, it's about time it opened." Abbey's eyes glistened, and for a moment he thought she might cry. "I was hoping she would tell you herself—thought it would be good for her to talk about it—but I don't mind spilling the beans."

"Are you sure?"

"Yes." She paused then started the story. "Daniel was Bree's sweetheart in high school. He was a quarterback on the team her father coached—their senior year."

"Wow. I would think having a player for a boyfriend would have endeared her to the game, not pushed her away."

"Well. . ." Abbey fiddled with the sheets then sighed. "From what I've been able to gather, my son has always been a tough coach. The players respect him, but he demands a lot from them. And everything came to a head during one particular game."

"Oh?"

"Mind you, I wasn't there that night. I only know what

I've been told. Daniel was playing really well, and they were leading. In fact, they were far enough ahead that the first-string should've been pulled."

"Right."

"Glen was trying to prove some sort of point to the opposing coach by running up the score, so he kept them in the game—well beyond the exhaustion point."

"Yikes. Dangerous."

"Right. From what I've been told, they were worn out by the fourth quarter. Daniel took a dirty hit late in the game, and they thought—at least at first—he'd broken his neck. Praise God, that wasn't the case. Several cracked vertebrae. But you know as well as I do what that meant for his career."

Brady knew, all right. All it would take was one more hit to a neck already damaged and the guy could be paralyzed for life.

"Daniel never played again. Never went to UCLA."

"Man, that had to be tough."

"Bree was devastated," Abbey added. "And Daniel was never the same after that, either. He pushed her away. I think he might've blamed her dad, and—from what I've been able to pick up—she did, too." Abbey's eyes misted over. "Her real issue has always been with her father, not football. It's funny how she has the two linked together in her mind."

A stirring at the back door startled them both.

"Bree," Abbey whispered then put her finger to her lips to bring the conversation to an abrupt halt. "She's home. I'll have to finish later."

"Okay."

Seconds later Brianna entered the room with three prescription bottles in her hand. She looked at Brady and offered him a curt nod. "Thanks for keeping an eye on things so I could do this. It put my mind at ease to know you were here."

"Sure. We had a great time."

"Brady's really lifted my spirits," Abbey added. "I was happy to have him. And I'm hoping he'll stay for lunch."

Brady looked at his watch, stunned to see so much time had passed. "Oh, I'm sorry, but I can't. The game calls."

"Then you must answer," Abbey said in a more-than-serious tone. "We can't have our star quarterback late for practice, now can we?"

He flinched at the words *star quarterback* but didn't argue. To do so would only add more attention to it, and that wouldn't bode well for him right now.

He nodded at Brianna as he made his way toward the front door. He wanted to pause, to take her by the hand and talk with her, to draw her into a quiet conversation, like the one they'd had at the hospital that day.

He couldn't seem to take his gaze off her, but she seemed distracted, distant, so he settled on a quick good-bye. "You ladies have a great day," he said with a smile.

Brianna offered a polite nod, and Abbey said, "Go get 'em, tiger!" then gave him a thumbs-up sign.

He swallowed the temptation to laugh and shot out the door, ready to face the rest of the day.

❧

The weekend passed uneventfully. Brianna fixed a couple of great meals, which Gran-Gran seemed to love. Several ladies from the church brought food, too, including Mitzi Meyers, the pastor's wife, who stopped by after church on Sunday. She prayed for Abbey and told her how much she'd been missed by everyone at Calvary Community.

On Monday morning, with Lora stepping in to care for her grandmother, Brianna finally felt free to return to work.

"Promise me you'll call if you need me for anything," she urged.

"Oh, go on now," Gran-Gran said. "It'll be good for you to get back to work. Besides, Lora's been itching to get into my kitchen to cook for me."

"I have?" Lora's eyes grew large. "You know I'm no cook, Abbey."

"Exactly. Which is why you need the practice. And I'll be here to guide you every step of the way."

Lora let out a groan, and Brianna giggled as she gazed at the two older women. She hoped when she reached their age she would have as much spunk.

A short time later, after weaving through morning traffic, she arrived at AB&D where her bosses met her with a dozen questions and a collection of cards for her grandmother. She responded to more than forty e-mails and several phone messages, though it took a couple of hours to do so.

At lunchtime her boss Roger appeared at her office door.

"Hey, Roger. What's up?"

"Just wondered if you wanted to grab lunch. Several of us are going out for Italian food."

"Ah. I wish." She leaned back in her chair and groaned. "But I'm so far behind on my work. And we have some pending accounts I might be able to acquire for the company if I play my cards right. *If* I move quickly, which means I'd better stay put."

"Okay." His gaze shifted to the ground, which struck her as mighty suspicious.

"All right, Roger," she said, looking him in the eye. "Out with it. Why do you really want me to go to lunch with you and the other guys? And be honest."

"Oh, well, we were just thinking. . . ." He squirmed a bit then shrugged. "We were kind of thinking you might want to share some info about Brady Campbell. He's lived next door to you for a few weeks now." His voice grew more animated, and his eyes lit up. "We all saw the articles in the paper and heard the story on TV, so we're dying to know what's up. We figured you had the inside scoop on the guy—that's all."

Brianna let out a groan. "I might've known this had something to do with football."

"Well, it doesn't *have* to be about that. But. . ."

"What?"

"Well, we were thinking—since you live next door to the guy and all—that you might throw a party or something and invite us over. To meet him."

"Are you serious?"

"Sure. Why not? And besides"—he gave her a serious look—"rumor has it he's thinking about buying a house in town in the spring, down in the Riverparc area or maybe even Firstside."

"Where did you hear that?"

"Read it in the paper. We're talking about a guy with lots of money here, Brianna. He's going to want a mega-house. Or condo. And we were thinking—"

"I could coerce him into becoming a client?" She crossed her arms in front of her and gave him her best I-don't-think-so look. "Is that it?"

"Well, what would it hurt to let him know you're in the construction business?" Roger asked. "Really?"

"You're shameless."

"Look—you know how important it is to acquire new clientele, especially before the winter sets in. If he buys one of the older houses near town, he'll need a major remodeling job, maybe even an addition. And if he buys a condo he's likely to need upgrades. So who better to serve his needs than AB&D?"

"Uh-huh." *So that's what this is about.*

"If we can get his endorsement for the company, business would soar through the roof," Roger argued. "And it's not like we'd be using the guy, not really. We'd do quality work, work we'd all be proud of, as we always do."

"Roger, tell me you don't mean it. You would *not* put me in this position. Surely not."

"Just tell him about our competitive prices and focus on the quality craftsmanship. I can put together a list of satisfied customers from our existing clients." On and on he went, singing the company's praises.

She finally worked up the courage to interrupt him. "Roger."

He backed out of the door, his hands in the air. "Just think about it. That's all I'm asking."

Brianna shook her head and looked down at the papers on her desk. She would not give Roger an inch on this one. If she did, he might take a mile.

After he left, she plunged into her work with a vengeance. His words fueled her, giving her an added motivation to work hard—to put this whole Brady Campbell thing out of her mind.

Moments later, however, she sat staring at the computer, unable to work. She gnawed on the end of a pencil until the eraser was nearly gone. She thought back over her earlier conversations with Brady, how she'd been swept in by his beautiful green eyes and his broad smile—not to mention his broad shoulders.

"I'm just like one of those cheerleader-type groupies of his," she acknowledged to the empty room. "I'm pathetic."

For a second—just a second—she let herself think about the possibilities of getting involved with someone like Brady. He had been great to—and for—her grandmother, hadn't he? And their prior conversations, particularly those at the hospital on the day of Gran-Gran's accident, had been very sweet, hadn't they? Surely he was just a normal guy, in spite of the media frenzy.

Just as quickly she remembered the newspaper articles, the stories of where he'd come from, the man he used to be.

Was Gran-Gran right? Had he really changed, or was he simply taking advantage of the media to make himself look good?

Hmm.

Maybe, in spite of all outward signs, he was just a man longing to begin again. And maybe she should keep her opinions to herself. . .and let him do just that.

sixteen

Several weeks went by, and Brady settled into a routine of daily practices and football games. Playing well became a top priority. After all, Pittsburgh was known for its quarterbacks, and Mack Burroughs seemed intent on adding Brady's name to the ever-growing list of greats.

"Pittsburgh is the Cradle of Quarterbacks, Campbell," Burroughs reminded him daily. "Some of the greatest men who ever played the game came out of the City of Champions, and you're going to be no different. You're going to shine like a star."

The idea of shining like a star held little appeal, but playing well did, so Brady spent hours each week perfecting plays, poring over the playbook, and working out with his trainer in the weight room. Between practices and games, of course. And all in an attempt to better himself. To make his new team proud. He nearly wore himself out in the process, but he knew it would be worth it in the end.

As for the players, most of the guys were fun loving and easy to get along with. A couple ran on the arrogant side, but that would pass with time. This he knew from his own history. And four of the guys on the team were strong Christians. One of them—Gary Scoggins—even invited him to church. Brady visited a few Sundays, then tried a couple of others, including Abbey and Brianna's church, which he loved. On those visits Brianna had been gracious enough to offer him the spot next to her.

One thing about going to church proved difficult. Thanks

to the recent media coverage, folks tended to greet him like royalty. One awestruck pastor even pointed him out to the congregation. Awkward. How he wished he could blend in for a change. Maybe with time.

Somewhere in the mix of all he had to do, Brady found time to slip over to Abbey's a couple of times a week for a gab session. And food. Always food. He enjoyed long conversations with her and kept a watchful eye on her healing process. The mending came slowly, but, thanks to physical therapy and lots of prayer, she seemed to be moving a little better. Surely by midwinter she would be back to her old self again. Maybe then he could invite her to a game and make sure she had one of the best private boxes in the stadium, where she could entertain her friends.

The weather in the Pittsburgh area shifted rather abruptly in late October, and by early November he experienced his first-ever snowfall. That same week he received a call from his mother. He predicted her opening line.

"I know, Mom," he said with a groan. "It's cold up there." They spoke the words in unison, but for once he didn't let them get to him. Undaunted by his mother's lack of zeal for his new home, he went on to sing Pittsburgh's praises. And he didn't have to exaggerate. In spite of the weather, he'd fallen in love with the city already, so much so that his desire to bring his mother there intensified with each passing week. The more he got to know Abbey, the more he felt sure she and his mom would be fast friends. Add Rena and Lora to the mix, and his mother would *have* to fall in love with Pittsburgh, cold or not.

"Let's see how you do this season," his mother finally agreed. "If it looks like you're going to be staying in Pennsylvania for more than one season, I'll agree to pray about it. But I'm telling you now—"

He didn't mean to interrupt her, but his response just slipped out. "Mom, I plan to be here for the rest of my career." Where the words came from, he had no idea. To be honest, as much as he loved his coaches and fellow players, he'd never really thought about living there for years to come. Most in his profession were usually itching to move on after a couple of seasons.

Still, it would be great to have his mother there, and he reiterated that point as he ended the call. He could see himself settled down with a wife and a couple of children, with his mom and Abbey nearby to watch over them.

Abbey?

Hmm. If he moved to Riverparc, like so many of the other players, he probably wouldn't see much of Abbey.

Or Brianna.

His heart grew heavy as he thought about her. For weeks she'd given him little more than a polite nod or a wave. Even when Abbey had invited him for dinner, Brianna had been noticeably quiet. He prayed she would let go of any pain from the past and give him a chance.

Truth be told, he cared about her. And he wished—he wished she cared for him, too.

The revelation had come over time as he'd watched the way she fretted over Abbey. As he'd heard her laugh with Rena and Lora. As she'd shoveled snow from the driveway.

As she had reached to touch his hand that day in the hospital.

Brady peeked out of his living room window and sighed as he saw the snow-packed front yard. His mom was right. It *was* cold up here. And, as he glanced toward Brianna's duplex, he realized. . .it was even colder. . .over there.

❧

By mid-December, Brady Campbell had drawn more attention

to the team than any other player over the past three years. Brianna tried not to focus on the newscasts, tried to avoid the in-office drama associated with all of the hype. But she had to admit, he had proven to be a great player.

This she noticed as she watched the games in secret in her bedroom.

Between practices he came and went from the duplex, though she had it on good authority—Gran-Gran—that he would soon be listing his duplex with a Realtor. For some reason, the thought of him moving away caused a tightening in her chest, one she couldn't seem to shake.

Gran-Gran would miss his visits, to be sure. She counted on his great stories and hearty laughter. And Rena and Lora would be devastated, too. If Brady moved away, they'd lose their claim to fame.

Brianna tried not to think about it. She also tried not to think about the rumors going around that local women now found him to be Pittsburgh's latest hot bachelor. With all the attention, would he slip back into his old ways? Brianna couldn't be sure why this bothered her so much. Likely because of his friendship with Gran-Gran.

Right?

She prayed about this very thing as she made her way to the airport the week before Christmas to meet her parents and her brother. She also prayed about her relationship with her father, asking the Lord to give her the right words to say in his presence and to relieve the feeling of pressure she felt in her chest every time he was around.

Brianna met her family in the baggage claim area with a squeal of glee. Her mother wrapped her in a warm embrace. So did Kyle. Her father seemed to be a little travel-weary but offered a loose hug. Maybe he was softening with time.

They arrived back at the duplex, where her mother scurried

into action, pouring her attentions into helping Abbey and cooking dinner. Both Kyle and her father seemed intent on meeting Brady, so Brianna slipped next door to see if he would be willing to stop by for a visit. Unfortunately he wasn't home. Then again, the Steelers were in the play-offs. Likely he was at practice.

She plodded back home, the bearer of bad news. Kyle seemed to take it well, but her dad looked disappointed. Still, he made polite conversation during dinner, asking Brianna about her job and telling Gran-Gran he would hire someone to paint her house once the spring came. Overall, things seemed to go a lot smoother than Brianna had expected. In fact, by the time the meal ended she felt a renewed hope that God could restore her relationship with her dad.

After polishing off some homemade banana pudding, she ventured into the living room ahead of the others to plug in the lights on the Christmas tree. The whole room seemed to come alive with color. This put Brianna in the mood for Christmas music, so she turned on the radio.

As the vibrant melody of "Carol of the Bells" filled the room, she found herself glancing out the window, looking toward Brady's place with a sense of longing. Had he even come home?

Nope. No car in the driveway. He was gone. For some reason she felt a twinge of disappointment. She had looked forward to introducing him to her family. Maybe she would catch him later in the week.

She sighed as she realized the truth of it. She missed him. Missed his funny jokes. Missed the way he always made Gran-Gran smile. Missed the way she felt whenever he was around, the fluttering in her chest, the sense of anticipation whenever he spoke, the glimmer in his beautiful eyes.

Brianna snapped back to reality when she heard Kyle's

voice nearby. "Let me ask you a question."

"Um. . .okay." She turned to face him.

"You're interested in Campbell, aren't you?"

"W–what?" She tried not to let her expression give her away. "Why would you ask that?"

Kyle shrugged and smiled. "Well, Gran-Gran said a few things on the sly, and the rest I figured out on my own."

"There's nothing to figure out," she snapped.

"Mm-hmm."

He planted a kiss on her cheek. "I believe you. 'Course, I used to believe in Santa Claus, too. And the tooth fairy. But what things *appear* to be and what they turn out to be are often two different things, aren't they?"

She reached over and gave him a sisterly slap.

"Hey, what's up with that?" he grumbled.

"Just watch yourself, oh, brother of mine." She flashed a warning look. "I've already got Gran-Gran trying to plant thoughts into my head. I don't need you doing it, too."

"Who, me? Plant thoughts in your head?" He chuckled then slipped his arm around her shoulder and pulled her into a warm hug.

Just then her mother called out, "Coffee, anyone?"

Brianna turned to see her parents entering the room. Her mom carried a tray of filled coffee cups, and her father followed along behind, holding the sugar and creamer. Gran-Gran brought up the rear, smiling as she inched her way along. Brianna couldn't remember when she'd ever seen her look happier.

As they settled in front of the tree, Brianna leaned back against the sofa and looked around the room.

" 'Tis the season," she whispered.

The season to begin again.

seventeen

The day before Christmas, weather forecasters predicted incoming bad weather. As much as Brianna hated for her family to leave early, she knew catching a flight before the storm hit was crucial. They said good-bye at the airport. Her mother held her in a lengthy embrace, and Kyle gave her a brotherly hug.

Ironically, her father glanced down at her with what looked like tears in his eyes. "I miss you, Bree," he whispered then planted a kiss on her cheek. She swallowed back the lump in her throat and told him she missed him, too. Then she slipped her arm around him and gave him a tight squeeze.

She pondered her father's actions for the rest of the day. Had she been wrong to hold him at arm's length for so long, to somehow pay him back for what had happened to Daniel? Was she still harboring unforgiveness, even after all the times she'd dealt with her feelings?

She fell asleep that night, thinking of the years they had missed, wishing she could make up the lost time.

The following morning she awoke to a white Christmas. Brianna and her grandmother opened gifts together mid-morning. A light snow covered the lawn, just perfect for Christmas Day. "That's one thing they never had in L.A.," Brianna said, pointing toward the window.

"Pretty, isn't it?"

"Mm-hmm."

They sat for a moment before Brianna remembered she had a turkey roasting in the oven. She scooted off to tend to their meal. After all, Rena and Lora would be here within the hour.

And Brady.

Why he had accepted her grandmother's last-minute invitation was a mystery. Now that he'd become the city's star player he could have had Christmas dinner with almost anyone. But Brady had chosen to spend this special day with them. . .for whatever reason.

A few minutes later Gran-Gran pulled Brianna into the living room. Her face wore a worrisome look, one Brianna didn't know quite how to interpret.

"Sit for a minute, and let's have a chat."

Brianna sat on the sofa and pulled a blanket over her feet. "What's up, Gran-Gran?"

Her grandmother's brows knitted, and her lips grew tight. "You know I'm quite a talker."

"Clearly." Brianna nodded with a smile.

"So I'd imagine that for me to say I'm going to have a little trouble sharing this story will put things in perspective for you," Gran-Gran said.

"Definitely."

"There's something I've been wanting to tell you," her grandmother whispered. "Had to wait till just the right time."

"And this is it? Christmas?"

"Well, Christmas, yes. And something else, too." Her grandmother's eyes took on a faraway look. "It has a little something to do with the fact that your father was just here. I've been praying the Lord will restore our relationship. Maybe this trip provided a start for that; it almost felt like it."

"I agree," Brianna said. "I felt the same way. So is that what you wanted to talk about? Dad?"

"Well, it's kind of a story that leads up to your father," Gran-Gran explained. "And I have to go backward in time to another Christmas season years ago. Do you have a few minutes to listen to an old woman ramble?"

"Don't be silly." Brianna snuggled in close. "I love your stories."

"Hmm. Well, this one begins in December 1941, just after the attack on Pearl Harbor."

"Wow. This is a *history* story."

"I guess you could call it that. It's the history of our family." Gran-Gran paused a moment then started. "I was just out of high school, and I'd fallen in love with a boy named Tommy. He was handsome, that boy."

Brianna giggled. "I don't think I've ever heard you talk about him."

"No, you wouldn't. Tommy was the first boy I ever loved, and I thought he hung the moon. I adored him. We dated the last two years of high school."

"Whatever happened to him?"

"Ah. He was drafted just out of high school. Went off to fight in the Pacific."

"Wow."

Gran-Gran's eyes misted over. "I loved that boy so much, and when he left it nearly broke my heart in two. We wrote letters the first few weeks, until. . ." Tears rose to cover her lower lashes, and she brushed them away with her fingertip.

"What, Gran-Gran? What happened?" Even before she got her answer, Brianna's heart grew heavy. This would not be a happily-ever-after kind of story.

"Bree, I'm not proud of what I did." Her grandmother spoke in a hushed voice. "I was just a girl in love. So in love I couldn't see straight."

"I'm not sure I know what you mean," Brianna said, reaching to squeeze her hand. "What did you do?"

Her grandmother's gaze shifted to the floor. "When Tommy

had been gone about two months I knew something was wrong. I could feel it. I didn't know anyone who had ever had a baby before, but I just knew. . . ."

Brianna's heart felt as if a vise grip had taken hold of it. "Oh, Gran!"

"I was a foolish girl, and I let my heart lead me into something that was wrong. Very wrong." She began to tremble at this point, and Brianna clutched Gran's hand as if her life depended on it. "Back in those days. . .well, it wasn't like it is today. Once a girl was found to be. . ." She didn't say the word, but she didn't have to. "Anyway, I waited as long as I could to tell my mother. She was devastated."

"I'm so sorry," Brianna whispered. "I'm sure it was a terrible time for both of you."

"Worse than you know." Gran-Gran shook her head, and a lone tear slipped down her cheek. "We got the news about Tommy when I was only four months along. He was. . .he was. . ." She covered her face with her hands and cried softly for a few moments then whispered, "He was killed in Bataan, along with thousands of other American soldiers."

"Oh, Gran, I'm so sorry! I'm so sorry." Brianna wrapped her grandmother in her arms. They sat together for what seemed like an eternity before she finally spoke. "W–what happened? What happened to you—and to the baby?"

"My parents didn't want anyone to know," she said. "So they sent me to stay with my aunt Nadine out in the country. She was my mom's youngest sister, not much older than I was, but happily married with a couple of kids of her own. Other than Nadine and the children, I didn't know anyone there," her grandmother explained. "It was a horrible, lonely time for me. Nadine and her husband wouldn't let me go anyplace, except to the tiny church they attended. But even there the lies were thick. She got a little wedding band out of a Cracker Jack box and put it on my finger—made me tell her friends and her pastor that my husband had died."

Brianna shook her head. "That's awful," she whispered.

"But then Katie came." Gran-Gran's face lit up at once.

"Katie." Brianna nodded. "I've heard you talk about her." She also remembered the photo on Gran-Gran's bedside table of the little cupie-doll girl with wispy curls and a winsome smile.

Her grandmother shook her head, and her hands trembled. "My parents wouldn't let me keep her. They told me I had to. . .to let her. . .go." The tears began again. "They made me leave her with Nadine to raise. I couldn't hold her, couldn't kiss her pretty little face, couldn't even let her know she was my own."

"But—" None of this made sense. "Everyone there knew you were the mother."

"Yes, but they went on believing the stories Nadine told them. She and my mother came up with what they thought was a foolproof plan. Nadine told her church friends I was too frail to care for the baby, too emotionally insecure. And, of course, my friends back home didn't know the difference. They didn't even know there *was* a baby. They just knew I'd gone to visit my aunt for a few months."

Gran-Gran paused and looked out the window as she whispered, "But *I* knew. I knew my baby girl had been stolen from me, and I prayed for her every single night." She paused, and some of the life returned to her eyes. "Nadine seemed to soften a bit over the next few years and even sent me pictures of the baby. She was gorgeous, a cherub, if I ever saw one. A real angel. I would hide those pictures under my pillow and cry myself to sleep. Then one day. . ."

A sinking feeling came over Brianna as her grandmother began to cry.

"We g–got the c–call on a Wednesday. Katie was just

three and a half years old, not even old enough for school. She'd been out in the field with my uncle, and there was an accident...."

Brianna squeezed her eyes shut, then let her own tears fall as her grandmother finished.

"She was riding the tractor with my uncle Raymond. She loved to ride up there. Loved it. But that day she. . .she slipped and fell and. . ."

Gran-Gran wept while Brianna held her close. She knew the rest already. No more needed to be said. Her grandmother had suffered enough already, and getting this story out had likely been the hardest thing she'd ever done.

After a few minutes of quiet mourning, her grandmother finally looked up at her.

"So now you know," she whispered. "You know—"

"That we both have things in our past we wish we could erase?" Brianna spoke over the lump in her throat. "That we've both needed—and received—God's forgiveness? That we've been able to forgive others?"

Gran-Gran nodded then reached for her hand. " 'All have sinned and fall short of the glory of God,' " she said quietly. "I can't tell you how many times I've quoted that scripture. And my other favorite one—the one about being cleaned as white as snow—"

" 'Cleanse me with hyssop,' " Brianna started.

" 'And I will be clean,' " Gran-Gran added. " 'Wash me, and I will be whiter than snow.' "

Yes, she knew that scripture well.

Something at the window caught Brianna's eye. Through the thin curtain she could see the sky, heavy and white. The bits of snow fluttered softly, slowly to the ground. She thought about them in light of everything her grandmother had said.

"Whiter than snow."

She turned back with a smile on her face. Suddenly she could hardly wait to see Brady.

✧

Brady arrived at Abbey's house at exactly 12:30 on Christmas Day—the appointed time. Brianna answered the door with a broad smile.

"Merry Christmas," he greeted her.

"Same to you. Come on in out of the cold." Oh, those words! They almost felt symbolic, as if Brianna were somehow declaring a truce, tearing down the wall that had risen between them.

She swung wide the door and ushered him inside. He shrugged off his coat, then managed to sneak a peek at Brianna out of the corner of his eye as he hung his coat in the closet. She looked especially pretty in that blue sweater. It really went well with her blond hair, which she'd swept up into a loose ponytail. And he liked her without makeup. No pretense.

"Well, hello there, Brady!" a trio of voices greeted him as he made his way into the kitchen. There his three biggest fans sat at the kitchen table, smiling.

"We're so glad you could make it," Abbey started. "How marvelous you didn't have a game today!"

"Amen to that." Brady chuckled at their enthusiasm. "And thank you for having me."

"Shame you couldn't go home to see your mama for Christmas," Rena said with a sympathetic shrug.

"Just before the play-offs?" Abbey exclaimed. "Are you kidding me?" She turned to face Brady. "Still, a good boy would've offered to fly his mama up for a visit at Christmastime."

Brianna chuckled from across the room.

"Oh, trust me." He raised his hands in the air for emphasis. "I've tried again and again to get her here, but I finally decided I should wait till spring. You'll just have to trust me on this."

He paused then rubbed his belly. "Something smells mighty good."

Brady could hardly understand a word after that. All of the women began to talk at the same time, each giving a dissertation on the food items she'd prepared.

Only Brianna, who'd started to slice the turkey, remained silent. He looked at her as she lifted the knife and gave her a warm smile.

When she returned the gesture, he walked over to her and took the knife from her hand.

"Allow me," he said with a wink.

She took a step back and shrugged. "Sure." Her cheeks flushed pink. "And thanks."

"You're welcome."

He went to work, carving like a pro. All the while he watched her out of the corner of his eye as she finished up the other dishes. At one point he almost got so distracted, the knife slipped.

Better watch what you're doing, Campbell. Don't want to lose a finger.

He gave Brianna another look, then turned back to his work, determined to stay focused.

Nope. Better not lose a finger. Not when he'd already lost his heart.

eighteen

January blew in with a vengeance, bringing a northeaster with it. Brady watched, astounded, as a blanket of white covered the whole city of Pittsburgh on the Saturday morning of a critical play-off game. He drove through heavy snow squalls, doing his best to maneuver the car on slick, ice-packed roads on his way to the stadium. Tree limbs, broken from the weight of clinging ice, littered the roadways. Even the rooftops seemed heavy with snow.

He half expected another one of those it's-cold-up-there calls from his mother, but he was thankful she held back.

Good thing, too. He would've had a hard time convincing her that this whole playing-in-a-storm thing was a piece of cake. In truth he was worried, not just about the journey to town, but today's play-off game against Denver, as well. Though he'd managed a couple of games on a muddy, snow-caked field, there was something to be said for indoor stadiums.

Still, he would give it his all.

By late morning, Brady arrived at the stadium and found the field to be mushy and white. He couldn't shake a stuffy nose and a lingering headache he'd had since practice, but he suited up as always. He went through the usual motions, even prayed with the guys before heading out of the locker room. As he jogged out onto the field with his teammates, the near-white field almost blinded him. The field wasn't just hard to see; it was particularly difficult to maneuver. Brady looked up at the skies and willed the snow to stop.

Moments later he stood on the sidelines, waiting for

the game to begin. Even with the warmers in his jersey, he couldn't stop shivering. Was it just the weather, or was he really sick? Regardless, he hoped the biting cold would dull to a chill once he started playing.

"You doing okay, Campbell?" Coach Carter asked.

"Yeah." He pressed his gloved hands together and worked them back and forth, back and forth.

"Careful with that." Carter gestured to Brady's fingers. "Don't rub your hands together between plays, even if you're cold. You'll lose your ability to coordinate them well later on."

"Ah." Brady had no idea what Coach meant but immediately stopped the rubbing.

"I see it happen all the time," Carter continued. "Players end up jamming fingers or getting stepped on." He slapped Brady on the back. "Just one more trick to playing in the cold. But you'll learn."

Yes." Brady nodded then looked up at the skies overhead. "I guess this would be a perfect opportunity to make good on that promise to melt the snow underneath my feet."

"Looks like it," Carter agreed. "Just do your best, son."

He nodded, and once he took the field, the roar of the crowd motivated him to jump in the game, regardless of the weather or the numbing headache.

The first quarter passed uneventfully. Whether it was the snow or a lack of the usual motivation, neither team managed to score.

By halftime the score was 6-3, with Denver taking the lead. The players drifted back to the locker room, clearly discouraged. Brady would have been, too, but by now the dull ache in his head had magnified. He pulled off his helmet and rubbed at his forehead to try to relieve the pain.

The coach sat the team members down and gave them a stern lecture. He focused on his offensive players, asking them to go the extra mile.

And that's just what Brady determined to do. He headed back out to the field at the start of the third quarter and played like a champ, headache or not.

Unfortunately Denver rose to the challenge as well. By the end of the third quarter, the score was tied, 21-21.

Coach Carter sent his men back out onto the field at the beginning of the fourth quarter with a rousing cheer and an insistence that they bring this one home. Less than five minutes later the snow began to fall in sheets. Brady could hardly see his hand in front of his face, let alone the ball flying through the air. He somehow lost his bearings at one point, jarred by the movement of a fellow player.

He felt disjointed, uncoordinated. It seemed the cold had a grip on his spine, causing his back to lock up.

"Not now," he grumbled. If he played his cards right, he still had one good play left in him this afternoon, one last chance to score. Then his team would end up on top and advance to play another game.

He shook off the headache as best he could and took advantage of an unexpected opportunity as they neared the end of the quarter.

Hurry, Brady—hurry.

He managed to snag the ball, then faced the monumental decision of passing it off to someone else or running it over the goal line himself.

With the torrent of white snow blinding him, he ran toward the goal, dodging opposing players at every turn.

At first.

He remembered every second of the play—his labored breaths, painful from the cold. His lungs, feeling as if they would explode. His head, feeling hot and heavy. Nearing the goal line with the ball clutched in his hands. Hearing the hopeful cheers from the crowd. Trying to slow his gait.

Everything after that seemed to move in slow motion.

Brady remembered colliding with another player. Heard the splintering sound of the impact. Felt a horrible jarring in his neck. Pondered why a jolt of electricity shot through him. Sensed his legs go numb. Wondered why the world began to spin.

After that everything faded to sepia tones. The rush of other players surrounding him brought a strange comfort. The appearance of the team doctor added a degree of curiosity. But the look of terror in Coach Carter's eyes threw everything into a tailspin.

Brady felt the oddest sensation of being the center of attention as paramedics rushed onto the field. He couldn't seem to get the shivering under control. He'd never felt such cold.

Through the fog Brady wondered, *Did I cross the goal line? Did I score?*

He also found himself wondering what his mother might be thinking. Was she watching the game?

"It's cold up there."

The shivering grew more exaggerated—from fear or the cold, he could not be sure. The pain in Brady's head intensified, and he tried to figure out why his legs felt like electricity still coursed through them. After a moment or two the pain dissipated, and he seemed to completely lose feeling in both legs.

"Son, can you hear me?" The paramedic looked at him intently, even snapping his fingers in Brady's face.

"S—sorry?" The roar of the crowd seemed deafening. Or was it whisper-quiet? He couldn't tell.

"Can you move your legs?" The paramedic shouted to be heard above the crowd.

"I—I. . ." Brady did his best to lift his right foot, but it refused to cooperate. Frustrated, he opted for his left.

Nothing.

The sting of tears in his eyes further blurred his vision. He shot out a prayer, not caring who heard. "Oh, God! Help me!"

He lay shivering for what seemed like an eternity before they placed him on a stretcher and loaded him into the ambulance.

Ambulance?

After that, everything faded to black.

ta.

Brianna heard the scream from the bathroom and ran out into the living room to see what had Gran-Gran and her friends so worked up. Her grandmother sat on the edge of her seat, and Lora paced the room, wringing her hands.

"What happened?"

Gran-Gran looked up with tears in her eyes and shook her head.

Brianna glanced at Rena, who appeared to be the only one in the room not falling apart. "*What* happened?"

"It's Brady," Rena whispered. "He's been. . ." She pointed at the television set, and Brianna dropped onto the sofa next to her grandmother to watch. What she saw took her breath away. Brady lay in the midst of a snow-covered field, completely still. A team of paramedics worked on him feverishly, though she couldn't make heads or tails out of his injuries.

Right away her hands began to shake. Bree grabbed one of the throw pillows from the sofa and gripped it as tears filled her eyes. She found herself caught up in a memory of the night Daniel had been injured. Her sobs had been deafening, even more than the ladies' were now.

And she had known. Known Daniel would never play again. Known her dad had been responsible. Known. . .

This is why! This is why I can't stand the game. Why does this always seem to happen to the people I love? Why do they always end up hurt?

She drew in a deep breath and tried to remain calm as the truth settled in her spirit. Daniel had recovered from his injuries—internally and externally. He'd gone on to live a normal, healthy life. Surely the Lord would do the same for Brady. Wouldn't He?

Brianna turned her attention back to the television set, watching as the paramedics lifted Brady onto the stretcher and carried him away in the ambulance. Her heart felt broken in two, and she reflected on her earlier thoughts: *Why does this always seem to happen to the people I love? Why do they always end up hurt?*

The *people* I love? *They?*

So this wasn't just about Daniel anymore.

This was about her love for Brady, too.

How had she pushed down the feelings that now consumed her? How had she gone this many weeks—months—and not been honest with herself about how she felt about him? Why did it take something this catastrophic to convince Brianna that her feelings for him were deeper than she'd dared dream?

Oh, God, please touch him. Heal him. Protect him.

Brianna covered her face with her hands and wept. Gran-Gran reached to take her hand. "I know, honey."

Just three words. But they said it all.

nineteen

The next day Brady lay in the bed, unable to think clearly. Results of the initial tests, CT scans, and MRIs were inconclusive. But after sixteen hours the feeling had returned to his legs. Thank the Lord. Brady didn't know when he'd ever been as shaken. Both his faith and his body had taken a tumble over the past day or so.

And all for a losing game.

He couldn't throw off the fact that he'd come so close—*so* close.

And yet so far.

The doctor—a fellow who had introduced himself as David Grant—entered the room with a nod and a hint of a smile.

"Good news, I take it?" Coach Carter asked from his chair next to the bed.

"Well, no breaks. Nothing permanent. What we're looking at here is what's commonly referred to as a stinger injury."

Brady nodded and remembered a fellow player in Tampa who'd been off his feet for days with a stinger injury.

"The nerves that give feeling to the arms and hands start out in the neck area." Dr. Grant reached to a spot at the back of Brady's neck. "Nerve injury often happens when the athlete makes a hard hit using his shoulder. The direct blow to the top of the shoulder drives it down and causes the neck to bend toward the opposite side."

"I felt it when it happened," Brady said.

"No doubt. We're talking about a motion that does a

133

whopper of a job stretching or compressing the nerves, to the point where it triggers a pretty intense discharge of electricity. For a few seconds the electricity shoots down the nerves to the tips of the fingers."

"Felt that, too. Just after the impact."

"In your case," Dr. Grant said, "the spinal cord in your neck was bruised during the impact, causing your whole body to be affected from the neck down, not just your arms. We see this occasionally, though it always gives the patient and the doctor quite a scare."

Carter stood and began to pace the room.

Brady watched his coach out of the corner of his eye as he propped himself up in the bed. He still fought a lingering headache. "But this isn't permanent, right?" he asked. He just needed to hear it again, to assure himself.

"Well, your symptoms—pain and tingling in both arms and legs—have passed," Dr. Grant explained. "There are no cracks. No breaks. Nothing like that. Once we have determined that your sense of feeling, strength, neck motion, and reflexes have returned to normal, you will likely be able to return to the game next season."

"Likely?" Carter and Brady spoke in unison.

"Look." Dr. Grant pulled up a chair next to the bed and took a seat. "I've seen this before—where an athlete has a stinger injury—then doesn't wait until he's completely healed before jumping back into the game. The goal here is to prevent a recurrent stinger. If you take another hit, your injuries will likely be more severe. We could even be talking permanent nerve damage if you're not careful. So no practices, nothing like that, for a while. We want to err on the side of caution. And I mean that."

"Right." Carter nodded. "And we put these guys through an exercise regime at the beginning of each season to develop full range of motion in those muscles. We'll keep a close eye on him, I promise."

"Good." Dr. Grant turned back to Brady. "In the meantime I'm referring you to an orthopedic doctor, and he'll perform a thorough evaluation of your neck, shoulders, and nerves."

"Here? In the hospital?"

"Nah. No need for that. Oh, and by the way—"

"Yes?"

"You have a low-grade fever. Have you not been feeling well?"

"I had a terrible headache last night," Brady said. "Felt a little woozy. And I've been kind of stuffy. I wondered if the shivering was from the cold or something else."

"Ah. Well, we've seen a lot of flu-type symptoms going around, so I'll put you on a decongestant for that. Could be that's what had you so off balance in the first place."

"Thanks," Brady said. Then with a sigh he leaned back against the pillows.

"Just so you know," Dr. Grant said with a sympathetic smile, "you've played great all season. Everyone in this city is proud of you. And right now they're just rooting for you to get better so you can come back next season."

"He's right, Brady," Coach Carter said with a nod. "That's the important thing here—getting you better. And not *just* because of the game."

Brady smiled his thanks.

"Okay." The doctor nodded. "I'm releasing you. Just make sure you have someone with you over the next few days. Head and neck injuries are nothing to ignore. You'll need to be watched."

"We'll make sure of that," Carter said.

"Okay, well, be looking for a nurse to show up in about an hour or so with your discharge papers. You can go ahead and get dressed if you like." He walked out of the room, saying something about writing a prescription for pain.

Carter gave him an inquisitive look. "You okay, son?"

"Yeah."

"I wanted to let you know the mayor called this morning to check up on you."

"He did?"

"Yes, and someone from the governor's office, too. They're all rooting for you."

"Wow." Brady shook his head at the thought of it.

"Of course, a dozen or so reporters are hanging around in the lobby of the hospital, so we'll have to make a statement on the way out. Just wanted to get you psychologically prepared for that."

"It'll be fine." Brady smiled.

"Great." Carter glanced at his watch. "I'm going downstairs and make a couple of calls before we leave. Just call my cell when they've discharged you, and I'll meet you downstairs to take you home. And don't worry—I'll make sure you get back and forth to your doctor's appointments, that sort of thing. We'll take care of everything. You just rest easy."

"Yes, sir."

Seconds later Brady found himself alone in the room— alone with his thoughts. He felt torn between being thankful God had spared him from a more serious injury and regretting that he'd fallen short of the goal line. He hadn't led his team to victory. For whatever reason, that brought on a nagging feeling of guilt. He couldn't shake it.

Then again, guilt seemed to be his middle name.

Maybe it had something to do with the call from his mother late last night. She'd been in quite a state, and he couldn't blame her. He knew how badly she wanted to come, but he'd insisted she not fly up there with the weather so bad.

Besides, he'd told her, he would recover within days. By the time she could travel, he'd be feeling great.

She promised to come in the spring, as soon as the snows cleared. He hoped the weather would cooperate; otherwise, he'd never live it down.

He thought about that for a while. Maybe he placed too much stock in what people thought, even people he cared about deeply. Maybe that's where the guilt came from—caring too much.

Or maybe he could blame it on the look in Brianna's eyes when she'd come by for an unexpected visit this morning. Just the idea that she'd forged through the storm to visit him had brought a sense of hope. . .expectation.

Brady closed his eyes and reflected on the pain in her expression. Looking at those eyes had convinced him of one thing.

She cared about him.

She didn't have to say it. Not yet, anyway. But he knew, as Abbey had said, in his knower. He knew Brianna had come to see him because she cared.

And soon enough, if the Lord continued to work in such a miraculous way, he would be ready to tell her how much he cared, too.

Brady smiled as he thought about their visit. So many good things had come out of it. For the first time in weeks they'd talked. Really talked. She had even shared a few tears and an apology.

He reflected on that part—how she'd finally told him her reasons for hating the sport. She explained about Daniel's terrible injury and the forgiveness she'd finally been able to offer her father after so many years of holding a grudge.

Her tears had flowed as she shared about her past and the changes she'd been through in recent weeks. Brady's favorite part was her embarrassed confession—what fun!—that she'd finally started watching the games—in spite of her fears that someone, like him, for example, might be hurt.

The look in her eyes as she'd gazed at him made every bit of the pain worthwhile.

Oh, how wonderful it had been to spend an hour with her, just talking—about their hopes and dreams. Their pasts. Their futures.

Brady's eyes opened, and he half expected to see her standing there beside him, her hand clutched tightly in his own.

If the Lord responded favorably to his prayers, one day she would be.

❧

On the day after Brady returned home from the hospital, Brianna took a meal to his home. She stood at his front door, bundled in her heaviest coat and clutching a plate of food in her hand. It contained several of his favorites—meat loaf, fried bread, and the creamiest mashed potatoes in town—and she was happy to deliver it. In fact, everything about being with Brady made her happy, and she was finally ready to admit it.

After a couple of knocks the door opened. Brianna gasped as she saw both of his eyes completely blackened.

"Oh! You look worse than you did in the hospital."

"Humph. I don't know whether to thank you or be offended," he said with a weak smile. He gestured for her to enter the house, which she did with a shiver.

"Hungry?"

"Always!" He took the plate from her and led the way to the kitchen, where he pulled back the plastic wrap, then looked up with a big smile. "Thank you so much."

He set the plate on the table and pulled out a chair for her. Brianna hardly knew how to react. How long had it been since a man had offered this gesture of kindness and chivalry? Ah, yes. Christmas Day. Brady had done the same thing when they'd shared Christmas dinner together. It had felt good then, and it felt even better now that they were actually alone together. She slipped into the chair, feeling more comfortable around him today than ever.

Brady took a seat next to her and looked back down at the food, his eyes lit. "A couple of the guys from the team stopped by with take-out last night," he said. "But it's not the same as Abbey's great cooking. This is certainly worth thanking God for." And he did. His prayer was simple and heartfelt. Afterward he took a bite of the meat loaf then sat back with a sigh. "Ah, yes. She's a pro. Gotta give her that."

Brianna finally worked up the courage to tell him something. "Actually I, um"—she did her best not to blush—"I made the food this time."

"Really?" He gave her an admiring smile. "Well, you've acquired her talent; that's for sure."

"You think so?" She watched him as he took another bite and nodded. "I've been working at it."

"It's great."

As he continued to eat, Brianna took silent assessment of his injury, at least the part visible to the eye. She wondered how deep the wounds went, psychologically speaking. This must be quite a blow, especially knowing he'd have to take it easy for a while. Should she ask him about it? With more sighs coming forth from him, she opted for Plan B: food and chitchat.

She would give her questions to the Lord as she lifted Brady's name in prayer each day. And she would also ask the Lord something else, too.

She would ask Him if He would give her the desires of her heart.

twenty

The following Sunday morning, after a week of snow, the city of Pittsburgh remained blanketed in white. Brianna wouldn't have gone to church, even if the weather had cooperated. She called the pastor's wife early in the morning to explain their predicament. Gran-Gran was sick. Really sick. She'd been fighting a cold for days, and it seemed to have settled into her bronchial tubes.

Mitzi prayed over the phone and let her know others would be praying. A second telephone call, this one to the doctor, relieved Brianna's mind a little. He'd been happy to call in some antibiotics to the pharmacy, but he cautioned her to keep a close watch on her grandmother. And that's just what she did.

Under other circumstances Gran-Gran would've laughed it off. She always managed to remain positive and upbeat, even in times of sickness. But this time she kept herself quiet and still under the bedcovers, coughing and trembling as the fever peaked. Brianna made sure she administered the medication every four hours, along with aspirin.

As she did she prayed fervently that the sickness wouldn't develop into pneumonia. She found herself given over to that concern, however, on more than one occasion. What would she do if she needed to get Gran-Gran to the doctor's office or the hospital in a hurry? The roads were in such a mess. Would she have to call for an ambulance?

About ten thirty in the morning, Brianna went into her grandmother's bedroom to check on her. She found her tossing and turning in the bed, clearly uncomfortable.

"Is there anything I can get for you, Gran?"

"Hmm? Oh, Bree, is that you?" Her grandmother looked up with glazed eyes. "I think I was dozing."

"You look a little restless to me," Brianna observed. "Can I get you something from the kitchen? Do you need some hot tea? Or maybe you're ready for some chicken soup? I've been downstairs cooking all morning."

"In a few minutes, maybe." Her grandmother sat up in the bed, and a coughing fit erupted. When she finally finished, she looked at Brianna and sighed. "I'm not having much fun with this."

"I hear ya. I've been praying. I know Brady is, too."

"Brady." Gran-Gran's eyes lit up for the first time that day. "How is that boy?"

"Oh, he's recovering slowly," Brianna said with a shrug. "I've been over to his house off and on, taking food."

"Caring for two invalids at once is a lot to ask from one girl," Gran-Gran said. "And you're a doll to do it. I know we're both grateful." She paused a minute and shook her head. "It's Sunday, right?"

"Right."

"I don't even know if I feel up to watching the next play-off game, to be honest."

"Whoa." Brianna sat on the edge of the bed and placed her palm against her grandmother's forehead. "You really are sick, aren't you?"

Gran-Gran nodded then looked toward the window. "Is it still snowing out?"

"No. Nothing since last night. But I watched the forecast on television this morning, and they're asking folks to stay put in their houses." Brianna glanced over at her grandmother's bedside table, her gaze falling on a tiny, framed black-and-white photo. She'd seen it hundreds of times before, naturally, but this time it seemed to affect her in a different way.

"You're looking at Katie." Gran-Gran's weak voice took her by surprise, and for a minute Brianna felt like a kid caught with her hand in the cookie jar.

"She was really pretty."

"You looked just like that when you were three," her grandmother said with a nod.

"I did?"

Her grandmother reached to pick up the tiny frame, which trembled in her hand. "I always imagined she would've turned out just like you if she'd lived. I just know she would have. And so many times. . ." She got choked up.

"What, Gran?"

"So many times I've thanked God for sending you here to me. He gave me a second chance with a little girl."

Brianna laughed. "Well, I wasn't exactly a little girl when I came to you, was I?"

A serious look came into her grandmother's eyes. "You were on the inside. You were a hurt little girl, needing someone to reach out to love her."

A lump filled Brianna's throat as she thought about that. As always, Gran-Gran had hit the nail right on the head, though this one carried a bit of a sting.

"I told you on Christmas Day that I've been praying the Lord will restore my relationship with your father," her grandmother said with a slight sigh.

"Yes."

"I've been praying the same thing for you, too—that God will restore *your* relationship with your father."

Brianna stood and began to pace the room. "It's not so bad. I mean, we're civil and all. You saw how it was when he was here. We didn't argue or anything. I think we're making progress."

"Right." Her grandmother paused for a moment before responding. "But a relationship—a real one—is more than distant, guarded conversations. A relationship is—"

"It's what *we* have." Brianna sat once again and took her grandmother's hand in her own, as tears dampened the edges of her lashes. "And, to be honest, my relationship with you has been the healthiest one of my life. You're my best friend, Gran."

"Same here, pretty girl." Her grandmother's hand trembled in her own. "But that doesn't keep me from longing for the same with my son. In fact, it makes me want it more—for both of us."

Brianna thought about that before saying anything. "What can we do?" she asked.

"Hmm. I've been thinking on that a lot. Prayer, of course. We'll continue to pray. But in order to achieve a genuine breakthrough, I think I need to ask your father for forgiveness."

"Forgiveness? For what?"

A single tear slipped down her grandmother's cheek, breaking Brianna's heart. What could Gran-Gran possibly need to ask forgiveness for?

"I started telling you a story on Christmas Day."

"Started?"

"Yes. Remember I told you I'd leave the rest for another day?"

"Ah." Brianna nodded as the memory surfaced. "I remember now. You did say that." She gave her grandmother an inquisitive look. "What's the rest of the story, Gran?"

"The part I left out was this." Her grandmother's eyes filled with pain. "After I lost Tommy and the baby, I was the emptiest, most brokenhearted girl I knew. I couldn't seem to relate to the other girls. They were silly and flighty and had never been through anything like what I'd been through." She sighed deeply. "And the worst part was, I couldn't even tell any of them. I cried myself to sleep every night. It was the only relief I was afforded. That, and of course forgiveness from the Lord, which came many years later when I finally gave my heart to Him."

Brianna reached to squeeze her hand.

"I want to tell you about how I came to be courted by your grandpa Norman," Gran-Gran said with a smile. "He was tall, dark, and handsome, just like you read about in books. Worked at the filling station."

"I never knew that."

"It's true." Gran-Gran's eyes lit with pleasure. "I'd go over there with my dad to gas up the car and buy a soda pop or candy bar, that sort of thing."

"So Grandpa was really handsome?" Brianna asked with a grin. She had a hard time imagining such a thing but didn't say so.

"Like a movie star," Gran-Gran insisted with a nod. "And for whatever reason he seemed to take a liking to me. I knew my papa liked that notion. He wanted me to marry. I think he felt sorry for me, though he never came out and said so."

"Oh, I'm sure he did."

"Norman was a nice man and had lived in our little town forever. He was just the right kind of boy for me, kindhearted and stable. From a nice family. We all went to the same church, attended the same functions, had so many things in common."

"So he asked you to marry him?"

Her grandmother smiled. "Well, after a proper courtship. We married in the spring of '47. Things were really good those first few years. But when you enter into a relationship with an untold secret like the one I carried, it's only a matter of time before things get sticky."

"So you didn't tell him about Tommy?"

"Oh, he knew about Tommy," Gran-Gran explained. "They'd

been friends. . .schoolmates. Norman didn't know about—"

"Oh." The baby.

She closed her eyes. "I wanted to tell him. I can't tell you how many times I started to. Especially after we'd been married a couple of years or so. He wanted a child, and I"—her voice broke—"I just didn't know if I could handle the idea. But I couldn't tell him why."

Brianna shook her head, trying to imagine how hard that must have been—for both of them.

"Your father was born in 1951," she explained. "He was a handsome boy, the spitting image of his father. And in my heart I loved him so much. But. . ." She shook her head. "I don't know how to explain it, but I just couldn't seem to get close to him." Her eyes flooded with tears, and Brianna's heart nearly broke in two.

"That's not unusual after losing a child, Gran," she whispered. "It's hard to show affection to the next one. I've heard about that."

"But it wasn't fair to him—or to your grandfather." Gran-Gran began to cry and then started coughing again. When she finally calmed down, she explained. "I loved your grandpa, even if it wasn't quite the same kind of love I'd had for Tommy. I was a wonderful wife. Did all the right things. Thought he would never find out, but. . ." She closed her eyes while more tears fell.

Brianna watched in silence, whispering a prayer that the Lord would get her grandmother through this. Somehow she knew cleansing would come with the telling of this story. And understanding. And hope for the future—for their family.

"It happened when your father was just a toddler," Gran-Gran whispered. "Your grandpa Norman was searching through the drawers in our dresser for a savings bond. He stumbled across my photo of Katie, the one my aunt Nadine had sent.

I. . .I. . ." She shook her head, and for a moment Brianna thought she wouldn't be able to go on. "I thought about lying to him. I knew my mother would expect me to. And my aunt, though she had softened. But I couldn't do it. I took one look at that photo in his hands and told him everything."

"W–what happened?"

Gran-Gran bit her lip and didn't say anything for a minute. Finally she said, "He handed the picture back to me, told me to destroy it. Said we'd never mention it again to another living soul. I couldn't tear up the photo, so I hid it away. But from that day on, things were never the same between us. He became angry, distant. We went through the motions of being a married couple, but in reality we were both so far apart."

Brianna could hardly imagine her grandmother living through such pain.

"It was all so sad." Gran-Gran drew in a deep breath. "Funny thing is, I really loved the man. Loved him till the day he died. And you can blame him for my love of football." A hint of a smile graced her lips. "It was the one thing we had in common those last few years. We'd sit together and watch the games, and for just a few hours we were close. We could talk together and laugh. When the game was on I almost felt like all was right with the world—that nothing had ever happened to pull us apart. And I think he felt it, too. In fact, I'm sure he did."

She leaned back against the pillows and closed her eyes.

"Do you need to stop for a while, Gran-Gran?" Brianna asked.

"Just one last thing I need to tell you," her grandmother whispered. "Your father. . ."

"Yes?"

"He never knew."

"About Katie?"

"That's right. He never knew about her."

Confusion filled Brianna. "But you've kept her picture out for everyone to see."

"No. Only here at the house. And he rarely comes here. When he does he never seems to notice—least he's never asked about it. I've needed to tell him for years. I really want him to know. I feel like I need to ask his forgiveness for not being the kind of mother he needed, for pushing him away as a youngster when I should have drawn him close. The Lord has forgiven me"—her voice broke—"but I need the forgiveness of my son. I need it something awful."

Brianna tried to think of something to say, but no words would come. So many things swirled through her head at once, and her heart seemed to be caught up in the confusion. Just when she thought she couldn't absorb one more thing, Gran-Gran's eyes fluttered open once again.

"Was there something else, Gran?" she managed.

"I was just thinking of Brady."

"What about him?"

Her grandmother let out a lingering sigh. "I know he has a rocky past, and I can certainly relate to that. I also see how much he regrets his mistakes. I'm sure he wishes he could do it all over again. I see regret written on his face every time someone brings up his days in Tampa."

Brianna's heart twisted inside her at these words. She had been so hard on Brady in the beginning. How she regretted that now.

"But when I consider the two of you together as a couple," her grandmother continued with a smile, "I feel so hopeful. You've already opened up and shared about your issues with your dad, and he's told you his mistakes and failures. You've both come clean. There are no untold stories, no lingering secrets."

Brianna nodded. "Right."

"That's the best way to start a relationship, honey. The only way. With honesty. Each of you coming into it healed and whole, completely forgiven. Knowing without a doubt that God loves you and has washed you clean—as individuals. When you do that, you stand the best chance for a long, happy life together, with God at the center of your union."

"Union?" Brianna whispered the word. "Do you think—?"

Gran-Gran smiled. "I've spent a lot of time with the Lord in the past few weeks, and I sense what He's up to. I'm just so glad to know He's already done a healing work in you—and in Brady. The hardest part is truly behind you."

"Mm-hmm."

The only thing Brianna could think of was the scripture her grandmother had reminded her of on Christmas Day— the one about being as white as snow, about being washed, made clean. She wanted to remind Gran-Gran of that but couldn't seem to speak.

She wanted something else, too.

For the first time in a long while Brianna wanted to pick up the phone and call her dad.

❧

Brady paced around the house late Sunday morning, restless. Every time he thought about today's play-off game between Denver and Cincinnati, he felt ill. *We should have been the ones playing today. I should have led my team to victory.*

He began to pour out his heart to the Lord, all the while circling the living room like a caged tiger, leaving track marks in the carpet. On and on he went, emptying himself of the frustration and eventually receiving much-needed peace in its place.

When he finally reached the point where he could think clearly, Brady picked up the telephone to call Brianna.

If he couldn't play the game, he would at least watch it— with the woman he loved.

twenty-one

Brianna took extra time getting ready for Brady's arrival. She planned to wear her pink sweater and jeans and put on the tiniest bit of makeup. Then she would warm up the chicken soup and rolls, just in case he hadn't eaten lunch. All of this she did with a renewed sense of anticipation. And a few butterflies. She hadn't felt this way since. . .

Hmm. She didn't recall ever feeling this way. But she certainly liked the way she felt.

With Gran-Gran sleeping upstairs, she and Brady would have a chance to settle down on the sofa side by side and watch the game. Of course, she was still on a learning curve where the plays were concerned, but surely he wouldn't mind that. He might even be grateful for the chance to share his expertise.

Just about the time she climbed out of the shower, the doorbell rang. "What?" He was early. Almost an hour, in fact. She scrambled into a robe, wrapped her hair in a towel, and sprinted down the stairs. When she inched the front door open enough to ask him to give her a few minutes, she came face-to-face with Rena instead.

"Afternoon, Bree!" Rena pushed the door open and gasped. "Oh, my! You're in your robe." She quickly shut the door behind her, almost dropping the Crock-Pot she held in her hands.

"What's that?" Brianna asked. She certainly hadn't been expecting a food delivery today. Perhaps Gran-Gran had arranged it without telling her.

"Beef stew. Thought it might make Abbey feel better."

"Well, I made—"

"I just know she loves my beef stew," Rena added. "And with the big game coming, she needs to keep up her strength in order to cheer with the rest of us."

Rest of us? "Oh, well, she's not going to watch the game," Brianna explained. "She's sleeping."

"What?" Rena's stunned expression spoke volumes. "I don't believe it. Abbey? Miss a play-off game? Impossible!"

"She's really sick," Brianna said. "And it's probably not a good idea for you to be here. Likely she's contagious."

"Oh, pooh. I've had my flu shot. And I never get sick anyway. I have the strongest constitution in town. It's all that starch I eat. Gives me a backbone. Now just let me get this off to the kitchen, and then I'll stay and watch the game with you."

"Well, I—" Brianna never had the chance to finish her sentence. Rena disappeared into the kitchen.

Brianna had just turned to sprint back up the stairs when the front doorbell rang again. She let out a groan, then inched the door open once more. This time she found Lora on the other side, clutching a large pan in her hands.

With a sigh Brianna swung the door open and ushered the woman inside. "What have we here?" she asked, though the smell gave it away.

"Corned beef and cabbage," Lora responded. "Best thing in the world for opening up the sinuses. Abbey will be well in no time."

No doubt. "Rena's already in the kitchen. I'm headed upstairs to get dressed. Brady's going to be here—"

A knock at the door interrupted her sentence.

"Would you get that?" Brianna whispered. "I have to get dressed."

"Of course, of course." Lora set the pan down on the coffee

table then turned to open the door just as Brianna disappeared up the stairwell. Her heart thumped like mad all the way up the stairs. She could hear Brady's voice as he and Lora shared their hellos. His boisterous laugh rang out through the house, and Brianna felt a wave of relief wash over her. Apparently he didn't mind that two elderly women would be joining them today.

Make that three.

Just as she neared the upstairs bathroom, Gran-Gran made an appearance in the hallway, dressed in her robe, her hair piled all topsy-turvy on her head.

"What are you doing up?" Brianna scolded.

Her grandmother gave her a puzzled look. "I heard voices. Woke me up. Thought maybe it was a heavenly choir. Gave me a bit of a jolt."

"Very funny."

"Who's here? And why?"

"Everyone and their brother." Brianna let out a sigh. "And they've come to watch the game."

"Ah." Gran-Gran nodded. "I forgot to uninvite the ladies. They always see a game as a standing invitation. Are you upset?"

"Nah. I suppose it just wouldn't be right without them." Brianna gave her grandmother a motherly look. "But none of this explains why you're up and about. You should be in bed."

Gran-Gran shrugged. "I'm feeling better. My fever broke, and that decongestant you gave me really worked wonders."

"Uh-huh. Sure it did." Brianna stood in the doorway of the bathroom, gazing into the red-rimmed eyes of the woman she loved more than almost anyone else in the world. She wouldn't argue with her about something as silly as a football game. If her grandmother wanted to watch the game, she would watch the game, no arguments.

"Kickoff is in twenty minutes."

"I know." Brianna laughed. "I'm trying to get dressed, but no one will let me."

"Please." Her grandmother gestured toward the bathroom. "Be my guest." She gave her a wink. "And while you're at it, wear your blue sweater."

"Blue sweater? Why?"

Gran-Gran gave a little giggle then added, "I have it on good authority someone thinks it brings out the color of your eyes."

"Aha." Her cheeks warmed, and she closed the bathroom door to avoid any further embarrassment.

Brianna spent the next ten minutes slipping into her clothes, blow-drying and styling her hair, and applying a bit of lip gloss. All the while she thought about Brady.

Hmm.

Maybe she'd better not think *too* much about him while trying to apply mascara. The trembling in her hands made for a messy application.

Still—she gazed at herself in the mirror. Could he ever really love someone like her?

Love. Hmm.

She stared at her reflection, noticing the peaceful expression in her eyes. Oh, how wonderful it felt. Then with a happy heart she descended the stairs. Brady met her at the bottom step, his eyes growing wide as he saw her.

"You look great," he whispered. "That blue sweater is—"

He didn't finish the sentence, but she didn't care. The look on his face told her everything she needed to know. She managed to whisper a gentle thank-you and found herself unable to look into his eyes without blushing. *I feel like a schoolkid.*

Oh, well. There were worse things.

Brady took her by the hand, a gentlemanly gesture, for sure, and helped her down the last stair. She took hold of his hand as if she wouldn't have made it otherwise.

"Where are the ladies?" she asked.

"In the kitchen, warming up the food." He laughed but never let go of her hand. "I peeked. We're going to have a, uh, rather unusual meal."

"I think the corned beef and cabbage threw us over the edge," she agreed. "But don't feel as if you have to eat any or all of it. They think you're pretty special whether you eat their food or not."

His fingers gently intertwined hers, and he gazed into her eyes. "What about you?"

Her breath caught in her throat as she pondered his question. Did he want to know if she thought he was special or—?

"What did you cook?" he asked with a wink.

"Ah." She grinned. "Chicken soup."

"Ironic."

"Oh?"

"I have a hankering for chicken soup today. Call it a coincidence."

"Mm-hmm. Sure."

Just then something distracted them. The sound of three elderly women coming down the hallway toward the living room, chattering all the way.

"D–did you h–hear that?" Rena asked, breathless. "We're missing the k–kickoff."

"Oh?" Brianna pulled her hand out of Brady's, but not before her grandmother took note of it. The look of pure joy in her eyes was worth any amount of embarrassment. "Seems we have a game to watch," Brianna said, gazing up into his eyes. "Are you ready?"

"I'm ready." He reached once more for her hand, and together they walked into the living room to join the others.

❧

Brady sat on the love seat next to Brianna for most of the game. Most of it. Part of the time he paced the room, talking to the television screen. Not that anyone outside of this living room could hear him, but it did make him feel better. And the women seemed to get a kick out of it. Once Lora even leaped into position, pretending to catch the ball in midair. He smiled.

He wanted Denver to win, naturally. Needed them to win. What good would it do for the team that had taken them down to turn around and lose to someone else?

Midway into the fourth quarter, with Denver lagging behind, something occurred to Brady. What did it matter in the grand scheme of things? A game won. A game lost. Wasn't God in control, and wouldn't He work it all together for His good?

As the game came to its woeful conclusion, the four women sat with stunned looks on their faces. Most stared Brady's way, likely waiting for a comment. For a moment not a sound was heard in the place.

Well, unless Rena chomping on potato chips counted. "Well, that's that." She stood and folded up the bag, closing it with a chip clip. "C'mon, everyone. Let's go into the kitchen and have some apple pie," she suggested. "It just came out of the oven and looks delicious. I'll even dish up some ice cream to put on top."

"In this weather?" Lora argued. "You want ice cream?"

"Of course! What good would apple pie be without it?"

"Rena," Abbey scolded, "you told me just this week that you were starting a diet."

"Yeah, I thought about it," Rena said with a shrug. "But

I've decided the older you get, the tougher it is to lose weight. By then your body and your fat are really good friends. And I've never been one to break up a friendship. You know that."

Brady tried not to laugh but couldn't hold it back for long. He was glad that within seconds everyone else joined in, even Rena.

"Well, you can't say I didn't give it some thought," she said with a shrug. "Now come on. Let's go get that pie."

Brianna and Brady followed the women into the kitchen where they all sat together at the table. Rena set the pie in the middle of the table and began to slice hefty triangles.

After swallowing down several bites of the warm cinnamony stuff topped with vanilla ice cream, an idea occurred to Brady, one he had to act on. He turned to Brianna. "Wanna go for a walk?"

"What? It's freezing outside. Are you sure? You've been sick."

"I've been well for days," he argued. "But if it makes you feel better, we'll bundle up. I just really need to get outside and walk."

"In the snow?" Rena said with a snort.

"Rena, leave them alone," Abbey instructed. She looked Brady's way and gave him a wink. "You kids go on now and take a walk. Don't mind us. We've got things to do."

"We do?" Lora asked.

"Yes." Abbey rose from her chair and grabbed some pens and stationery. "We're writing letters to every player on the Pittsburgh team, congratulating them on such a good season." She looked up at Brady with a big smile. "Will you make sure they get them?"

"I will." He nodded, then followed Brianna as she rose from the table and headed toward the coat closet. Once there she slipped on a heavy winter coat, gloves, a scarf, and a hat.

He did the same, and within minutes they found themselves out on the sidewalk, easing their way through the white drifts that threatened to end their walk even before it began.

Finally they settled into an easy stride, only occasionally pausing to step over a patch of ice. Brianna pointed to the western sky. "I always think the sunset is prettier when the ground is covered in white."

Brady paused to look at it then nodded. The whole yard seemed to reflect the red-orange glow of the setting sun. He glanced back into Brianna's eyes, and she gave him a warm smile.

An invitation perhaps?

He reached for her hand, and she took it willingly. Even with gloves on he still felt the connection, still marveled at the fact that they had finally reached this point—where they knew they were falling in love.

They enjoyed a comfortable silence for a while before Brianna asked him a question. "How are you really feeling about everything that's happened over the past couple of weeks? And be honest."

"Well. . ." He paused to think about it. "Every player dreams of making it to the Super Bowl. But not every team can win every time. That's just the way it goes. It doesn't mean the Lord has suddenly stopped blessing my team when we lose a game; at least that's the way I look at it. I think maybe some of the guys on the other team just needed a boost."

She stopped walking and gave him an admiring look. "You're taking this really well."

He gazed into her eyes. "I have everything a man could ask for and more."

"Oh?"

He nodded. "I feel like the most blessed man on the planet this evening—championship or no championship." He gave her hand a squeeze, and she gazed up into his eyes with a hint of a smile on her face.

"Do you really mean that?" she whispered.

As he nodded, a light wind pulled a loose hair into her face. They both reached up at the same time to brush it aside. As their gloved hands met, Brady felt a rush of joy, sensing what was coming. He ran his fingertip lightly across her cheek, and she leaned into his palm and closed her eyes.

A cold wind blew around them then, and Brady remembered his mom's words: "*It's cold up there.*"

But as he leaned in to kiss Brianna, to whisper words of love into her ear, he had to conclude—there was nothing cold about it.

twenty-two

On a Tuesday in late April, Brady drove to the airport with anticipation mounting. How long had he waited for this day? Months! Finally, finally, his mom was coming for a visit.

He met her inside at the baggage claim area. Brady laughed as he saw her approaching in her heavy winter coat, wool scarf, and mittens. The hot-pink hat topped off the ensemble. He gave her a bear hug, lifting her off her feet as he often did. "It's about time. I'm so glad you're here!"

"Brady, put me down. People are watching."

"Aw, what do we care?" In truth he'd gotten used to people snapping his photograph in public places, so if any paparazzi happened to be hanging about, they could snap their cameras at will. He truly didn't mind.

Then again maybe his mama did. He loosened her from the embrace and looked at her with a smile.

They gathered her bags then headed out to the parking garage. She gave the blue skies an accusing look and yanked the scarf from around her neck. "Well," she grumbled. "It's downright warm here."

"It's nearly May. What were you expecting?" Brady laughed as he pulled her two rolling suitcases in the direction of the car. Once they were settled inside, his mom pulled off her hat and gloves. She spent a few minutes catching him up on life in Florida, especially concerning his older brother.

"God has been doing a real work in Patrick's life over the past couple of weeks," she said.

"Oh?"

"I think we're seeing a real turnaround. And he's been calling me—a lot."

"It's all those prayers you've prayed," Brady said. "They're powerful."

"They are indeed." She gazed out of the window with a look of wonder on her face. Finally, for some unknown reason, she turned and punched Brady in the arm.

"W–what was that for?" he stammered.

"Flowers are blooming on the side of the highway."

"Uh, okay."

"Flowers."

He wasn't sure what that had to do with anything.

"Just like we have in Florida. And look at that—" She pointed off in the distance at the hills. "Why, that's about the prettiest thing I've ever seen. This place isn't at all like you made it out to be."

"What *I* made it out to be?" Brady erupted in laughter. "Mom, you're a hoot. A hoot. But I love you."

She looked at him with an admiring smile. "Yeah. I love you, too, kid. I don't think I tell you that enough." She paused, and then she was all business. "Now tell me—have you made up your mind how you're going to do it?"

"Yep." Brady nodded. "We're going to her office."

"You're proposing at her office?"

Brady's heart swelled at the word *proposing*. From the minute he'd made the decision, he hadn't been able to wipe the smile off his face. And he had the perfect plan for how to go about it. Oh, sure, his buddies had suggested waiting till the new season—flashing BRIANNA, WILL YOU MARRY ME? up on the scoreboard. But he had something a little more private in mind.

Hmm. Maybe *private* wasn't the best word, considering all the people who'd be there. He looked at his mom with a smile. "I'm not actually going to propose at the office. It's just that she's expecting me there for a meeting. I've hired her firm to renovate my new place. They're upgrading the kitchen and bathrooms and replacing all the light fixtures, that sort of thing."

"Ah. So we're picking her up and going over there?"

"Yes." He smiled. "But I've already been there. All morning, in fact. I fixed up the balcony with candles, roses, music. It's gorgeous. And I have the prettiest view, so it just seemed like the perfect place. If she says yes."

"If?" His mom gave him a reassuring look. "She'll say yes. If she's half the woman you say she is."

"Oh, trust me—she's probably double the woman I say she is." Brady grinned. "I don't think the dictionary has enough words to describe how wonderful she is."

"Well, then, I feel better about letting her have you. I couldn't have parted with you to just anyone, you know."

"I know. But, Mom, you're going to love her. I know you are." He thought back to what he'd been saying before. "If she says yes, I'm hoping we can get married in the summer, right after the renovations are finished on my new place."

He could see them there—married. Raising a family.

With all his heart he could see it.

❧

Roger Stevenson appeared at Brianna's door with a smile on his face. "Hey."

"Well, hey to you, too." She yawned and leaned back in her chair. "What's up?"

"Oh, nothing much. Just wanted to make sure you remembered we're all going over to Brady's condominium to make some decisions about additional design features. He wants your input."

"Right." She smiled as she thought about Brady's inexperience with home remodeling and his insistence that she play a major role in all the selections, right down to the granite countertops and stone floor in the kitchen. "He's on his way here now to pick me up."

She'd no sooner said the words than Brady appeared behind Roger. Her boss shook his hand, then agreed to meet them in the lobby in ten minutes.

Brianna stood and gave Brady a warm hug as he entered the office. "Hi there."

"Hello to you, too." He gave her a tender kiss, one now so familiar that she didn't know how she'd ever lived without it.

Brady flashed a suspicious smile. "I want you to meet someone." He stepped back outside the door and reentered with an older—very tanned—woman in a bright pink T-shirt and jeans. She looked oddly familiar. Hmm. Might be the emerald-green eyes. They matched Brady's exactly. Unless the crinkles around the edges counted. And the wide smile was familiar, too.

"You're—you're—" Brianna couldn't seem to get the words out.

The woman pushed her way past Brady and grabbed Brianna like a long-lost child. "You're Bree!" she squealed. "I've heard your name a thousand times if I've heard it once."

"And you're Cora." *Why didn't Brady tell me you were coming?*

"I am." The woman took Brianna by the hands, then stepped back to look her over from head to toe. "So you're the little darling my boy has fallen in love with."

Brianna felt her cheeks flush but nodded anyway. *I love him, too. More than anyone will ever know.*

"Well, let me tell you a thing or two about him," Cora said. "For instance, did you know he snores?"

"Mom." Brady crossed his arms and gave his mom a pretend warning look.

She waved him away then added with a whisper, "Like a

freight train. And he leaves his socks on the floor."

Brady slapped himself on the head. "What are you trying to do, drive her away?"

"And," his mom continued with a gleam in her eye, "he's notorious for remembering people's birthdays and also for showing up unexpectedly with flowers in his hand for no good reason."

Brianna laughed. "So I've discovered. But I think I can live with that one."

Cora wrapped her in a motherly embrace, which she returned with a smile. She loved this woman already. But why was she here? And why didn't Brady tell her she was coming?

Brianna glanced up at the clock on the wall, then reached for her purse. "Roger's probably already headed down to the lobby. Are you ready to go?"

"Oh, I'm ready, all right." Brady gave her a wide smile, and the sparkle in his eyes stopped her.

Yes, he appeared ready.

But she wasn't quite sure for what.

twenty-three

Brady's mind reeled as he drove toward the condominium with both of the ladies chattering away. They didn't seem to notice his nervous condition. Good thing. He put his hand on his pocket for the hundredth time to make sure the box hadn't fallen out.

Nope. Still there. Just like the last time he'd checked. And the time before.

He went over the plan of action in his head, strategizing about how he would call her out onto the balcony to talk about patio furniture or some such thing. How he would drop to one knee and take her hand. How she would look down at him with a look of astonishment on her face.

His heart beat double-time as he thought about the suggestions his team members had made for what to say first.

"Tell her she's your first draft pick."

"Write *Will You Marry Me?* on a football and toss it to her."

"Ask her if she'll wear your jersey. . .for the rest of her life."

Brady chuckled, almost forgetting where he was.

"Everything okay?" Brianna looked at him.

He smiled and nodded. "Just thinking."

"Well, a penny for your thoughts then. I want to smile like that."

I hope you will. Soon.

He was thankful his mother—God bless her—swept Brianna up in yet another conversation. He would have to remember to thank her later.

In the meantime he'd better get back to making plans.

And quick.

⁂

So many things about this day just didn't make sense.

Why Brady's mom showed up unannounced.

Why John and Roger Stevenson both insisted upon following them to the condominium to oversee the changes. They rarely got this involved.

Why Brady couldn't seem to stop smiling.

Why she had the uncanny sense something huge was about to happen.

They arrived at the condominium, and Cora chatted like a schoolgirl as they made their way to the front door where they were greeted by—Gran-Gran and her friends?

Okay, this is weird. Brianna turned to give Brady a questioning look. "What's going on?"

He shrugged. "I wanted them to meet my mom."

Hmm. Well, that *almost* made sense, though they certainly could have met later—at the duplex.

As they stood outside the front door, the proper introductions were made. Brianna could tell right away that her grandmother and Cora would be fast friends. They started an animated conversation, one she couldn't keep up with if she tried.

Even on a normal day. When things weren't so out of kilter.

Brady's hand appeared to be trembling, and he fumbled with the key in the lock.

"You okay?" she whispered.

He nodded, but his pale complexion said otherwise.

"Are you sick?"

"No, I, um. . .come on in." He ushered everyone inside, but Brianna remained behind with him.

"Brady, I'm worried about you. You're not telling me something."

"What makes you think that?"

"Well, for one thing, the fact that you look as if you're about to lose your breakfast. And for another—" Just then she glimpsed the inside of the condo. "Wow. They've already started working. I didn't realize." She swept past him and went to examine the kitchen, which was nearly finished. "How—?"

Roger entered, followed by his brother. "Brady wanted a rush job, so we've been on it for days."

"But I thought"—she turned to look at Brady—"I thought we were here to finish choosing materials today."

"Actually we're here because there's something I need to ask you."

"About the condo?"

"No." He gave her a faint smile and took her by the hand. *Why is his hand shaking?*

Brady led her up the stairs and through the master bedroom, where he drew back the vertical blinds covering the sliding glass door that led to the balcony. Brianna gasped. The roses. The candles. The twinkling lights. They could mean only one thing.

"Brady," she whispered, then turned with tears in her eyes.

He slid open the door and ushered her outside. "After you." He gave her an impish smile, then looked out across the city. "I have the best view in town."

"Yes." She could hardly keep her emotions under control. "You're right about that."

"I can see myself out here in the morning with a cup of coffee."

"Mm-hmm."

"With you by my side."

"What?"

She turned to discover he had dropped to one knee. Tears rose to cover her lashes. "Oh, Brady."

"I love you, Bree," he said softly, taking her hand. "You're the best thing that's ever happened to me. And I know you're the reason God brought me here to Pittsburgh."

She tried to speak but couldn't. The lump in her throat wouldn't allow it.

He gazed up into her eyes and smiled. "I told you I have the best view in town, and I do. It's right here in front of me. If I could spend every morning of my life waking up to that smile—those eyes—that beautiful heart—I'd be the happiest man in town."

She nodded and managed to whisper, "I love you, Brady."

His eyes filled with tears, and he reached into his pocket, drawing out a tiny box. Her heart beat faster as he popped it open to reveal a large, exquisite marquise diamond in a white gold setting. Could this really be happening?

"I love you, Bree. I think I've loved you from the first day I saw you outside the duplex. And I've loved you more with every passing day. The more I get to know you, the more there is to love. You're the most giving, caring person I've ever known."

No, you are.

He grinned and gave her an innocent pleading look as he stammered the rest. "Will you—would you do me the honor of marrying me?"

She hardly remembered saying yes, barely remembered the feel of the ring as he slipped it on her finger.

What *would* stay with her—for the rest of her life—was the cheer that went up from the other side of the open sliding glass door.

epilogue

On a Saturday afternoon in mid-July Brady suited up—not in his football uniform, but a tuxedo. He turned to Gary Scoggins, football player turned groomsman, for assistance. As always he was full of sage advice.

"Shake off the nerves, Campbell," Scoggins instructed. "No point in getting tensed up before the big game." He laughed as he realized his mistake. "I, uh, I mean big *day.*"

"Okay." Brady went through a couple of his usual warm-up routines, though it proved to be difficult in a tux. His heart swelled with joy as he thought about all the Lord had done over the past several months. Seemed as if he'd lived in Pittsburgh forever.

His heart raced at the thought of marrying Brianna. *Why have You blessed me so much, Lord? You know my history. You know where I've come from. What did I ever do to deserve her?*

The answer came in the form of a gentle reminder that he was not the man he used to be. Not even close.

He glanced up at a sign on the wall, one he'd read dozens of times during the season: THE GAME OF LIFE IS A LOT LIKE FOOTBALL. YOU HAVE TO TACKLE YOUR PROBLEMS, BLOCK YOUR FEARS, AND SCORE YOUR POINTS WHEN YOU GET THE OPPORTUNITY.

Ironic. Especially when he considered the fact that they were getting married on the fifty-yard line.

A rap on the locker room door caused him to turn around. Brady's mouth dropped open when he saw his older brother standing there, looking spiffy in his black tux. Their mother stood at his side.

"I don't believe it!" Brady exclaimed. "I thought you said you couldn't come."

Patrick shrugged as he entered the room. He sauntered Brady's way and extended his hand. Brady took it. For a second. Then he grabbed his big brother and gave him a bear hug.

"I'm so glad you're here. It means so much to me."

"Well, I heard you needed a best man."

"You heard right." Brady glanced over at his mother, who looked stunning in her light blue dress. She moved in his direction, and he leaned down to whisper, "Thanks." Then he gave her a soft kiss on the cheek.

"No, I'm the one who's thankful," she whispered back. "You've done so much for me."

"Done so much?" What had he done, after all? Introduced her to three of the goofiest women he'd ever met? Watched as she'd fallen in love with the church—and the city? Moved her into his old duplex? Spiffed up the place to suit her taste? Created an opening between her side and Abbey's since they spent nearly every waking moment together anyway?

"Just one thing, Brady," she said, as she stepped back to give him a once-over.

"What's that?"

She pulled a paper fan out of her purse and waved it back and forth in front of her face. "Why didn't you tell me it was so hot in Pittsburgh?"

The laughter that followed was probably heard out on the field.

❧

Brianna primped in front of the full-length mirror, amazed at the fairy-tale-like quality of the white gown and tiara. She truly felt like a princess. Her mother leaned over to insert another bobby pin to hold the veil in place.

Brianna heard a sniffle and turned to see who had walked in the room. She looked up into her father's tear-filled eyes and smiled, not just because he'd flown from L.A. to Pittsburgh to walk her down the aisle, but because the Lord had done such a marvelous work in their relationship over the past few months. Their weekly calls had progressed from awkward to genuine and heartfelt. And the fact that they had openly discussed the past—asking for and receiving forgiveness from one another—had sealed the deal.

Well, that and the fact that she'd fallen in love with a football player. Her father was more than a little happy to be getting a quarterback for a son-in-law, though he never came out and said so.

Not that Brianna minded. Her days of football angst were definitely behind her. No twinges of doubt left. She would start the new season as Pittsburgh's biggest fan.

A strain of music drifted in from outside, and Brianna looked up, startled. "Is it time already?"

"They told us to listen for the Vivaldi piece," her mom said. "So I'd better go take my seat. I'll see you in a few minutes!" She leaned over and gave Brianna a kiss on the cheek. "I love you, babe. And I'm so proud of you."

Brianna looked around the locker room, suddenly alarmed. "Where's Gran?" She couldn't get married without her matron of honor, now could she?

"I think she's disappeared on us," Brianna's father said.

Her grandmother appeared, right on cue. "Sorry, sorry! I had to make one more trip to the little girls' room, just in case. Thanks for waiting." She let out a giggle. "Nerves, I guess. I've waited all my life to step onto this field, but I never dreamed it would be for a wedding."

Brianna laughed. Leave it to her grandmother to make this entertaining.

"Do you think I look okay?" Gran-Gran asked as she joined her at the mirror.

"You're prettier than the bride," Brianna said.

"Oh, posh. Now that's just ridiculous." Her grandmother stepped up for a closer look, dabbing at her lipstick. "But I do look pretty good if I do say so myself."

"Yes, you do." In fact, she looked amazing in her sky-blue dress. But there was something more. Gran-Gran glowed with both an inner beauty and an outer one. Now that was something one couldn't buy in a bottle or spread on with an applicator. No, this was a true-to-the-heart kind of beauty.

They stood, side by side, gazing into the mirror. In so many ways, Brianna saw herself in her grandmother's reflection, and vice versa. That revelation almost brought tears to her eyes. She couldn't think of anyone she'd rather be like than the woman who had poured so much into her.

Gran-Gran yanked up her skirt a few inches and fought with her slip. "Crazy thing," she muttered. "Hope it stays in place."

Brianna chuckled. "I certainly hope so, too. I can see the headlines now."

"Oh?" Her grandmother looked up, intrigued. "Do you think I'll make the papers again?"

"Well, not for *that*, I hope," Brianna said with a smile.

A shift in the music let them know the time had come. Abbey led the way, and Brianna followed behind on her father's arm. They made their way out of the locker room and onto the ball field, where rows of chairs had been strategically placed facing the fifty-yard line.

Even from quite a distance she could see Brady standing next to Pastor Meyers, waiting for her at the center of the field. A man who looked suspiciously like him stood to his left.

So Patrick came, after all.

Surely Cora had a hand in that. But how wonderful that Brady was finally able to communicate with his brother again.

She squeezed her dad's arm, and he glanced her way. "Doing okay?" he whispered.

Her eyes filled with tears, but she nodded anyway. When she thought back to that wounded young woman who'd boarded the plane to Pittsburgh years ago—when she reflected on how far she'd come—she couldn't help but cry.

She brushed back the tears and watched as Gran-Gran made the trip up the aisle on Gary Scoggins's arm. Sure, she moved a little slow, but everyone in attendance seemed quite taken with her, something Brianna knew she loved. As her grandmother took her place at the front on the pastor's right, Brianna's gaze landed on Brady. He looked stunned as he saw her for the first time in her wedding gown.

The bridal march began, and the moment she had waited for all her life arrived at last.

"Are you ready?" her father whispered.

She nodded, and they started the rehearsed march toward the fifty-yard line. Right, together. Left, together. Right, together. Left, together.

Oh, forget that.

"Can we pick up the pace?" she asked her dad with a wink.

When he nodded, she hiked her skirt up a couple of inches and sprinted—sprinted toward the goal.

A Letter To Our Readers

Dear Reader:

In order that we might better contribute to your reading enjoyment, we would appreciate your taking a few minutes to respond to the following questions. We welcome your comments and read each form and letter we receive. When completed, please return to the following:

Fiction Editor
Heartsong Presents
PO Box 719
Uhrichsville, Ohio 44683

1. Did you enjoy reading *White as Snow* by Janice A. Thompson?
   ❑ Very much! I would like to see more books by this author!
   ❑ Moderately. I would have enjoyed it more if

   _____

   _____

   _____

2. Are you a member of **Heartsong Presents**? ❑ Yes ❑ No
   If no, where did you purchase this book? _____

   _____

3. How would you rate, on a scale from 1 (poor) to 5 (superior), the cover design? _____

4. On a scale from 1 (poor) to 10 (superior), please rate the following elements.

   _____ Heroine   _____ Plot
   _____ Hero   _____ Inspirational theme
   _____ Setting   _____ Secondary characters

5. These characters were special because? _____

_____

_____

6. How has this book inspired your life? _____

_____

_____

7. What settings would you like to see covered in future
   Heartsong Presents books? _____

_____

_____

8. What are some inspirational themes you would like to see
   treated in future books? _____

_____

_____

9. Would you be interested in reading other **Heartsong
   Presents** titles? ❏ Yes ❏ No

10. Please check your age range:
    ❏ Under 18   ❏ 18-24
    ❏ 25-34   ❏ 35-45
    ❏ 46-55   ❏ Over 55

Name _____

Occupation _____

Address _____

City, State, Zip_____

OKLAHOMA
Weddings

3 stories in 1

In Oklahoma, a ranch becomes a haven from turmoil. The Curly-Q ranch is an oasis in modern Oklahoma for three people who carry a burden of responsibilities.

Contemporary, paperback, 352 pages, 5³⁄₁₆" x 8"

_____

♡

HEARTSONG
PRESENTS

If you love Christian romance...

$10.99

You'll love Heartsong Presents' inspiring and faith-filled romances by today's very best Christian authors. . .Wanda E. Brunstetter, Mary Connealy, Susan Page Davis, Cathy Marie Hake, and Joyce Livingston, to mention a few!

When you join Heartsong Presents, you'll enjoy four brand-new, mass market, 176-page books—two contemporary and two historical—that will build you up in your faith when you discover God's role in every relationship you read about!

Imagine. . .four new romances every four weeks—with men and women like you who long to meet the one God has chosen as the love of their lives...all for the low price of $10.99 postpaid.

Mass Market 176 Pages

To join, simply visit www.heartsong presents.com or complete the coupon below and mail it to the address provided.

✂ -

YES! Sign me up for Heart♥ng!

NEW MEMBERSHIPS WILL BE SHIPPED IMMEDIATELY!
Send no money now. We'll bill you only $10.99 postpaid with your first shipment of four books. Or for faster action, call 1-740-922-7280.

NAME_____

ADDRESS_____

CITY_____ STATE _____ ZIP _____

MAIL TO: HEARTSONG PRESENTS, P.O. Box 721, Uhrichsville, Ohio 44683
or sign up at WWW.HEARTSONGPRESENTS.COM